THE HUMANZEE EXPERIMENTS

THE HUMANZEE EXPERIMENTS

TERRY PERSUN

WILDBLUE PRESS

WildBluePress.com

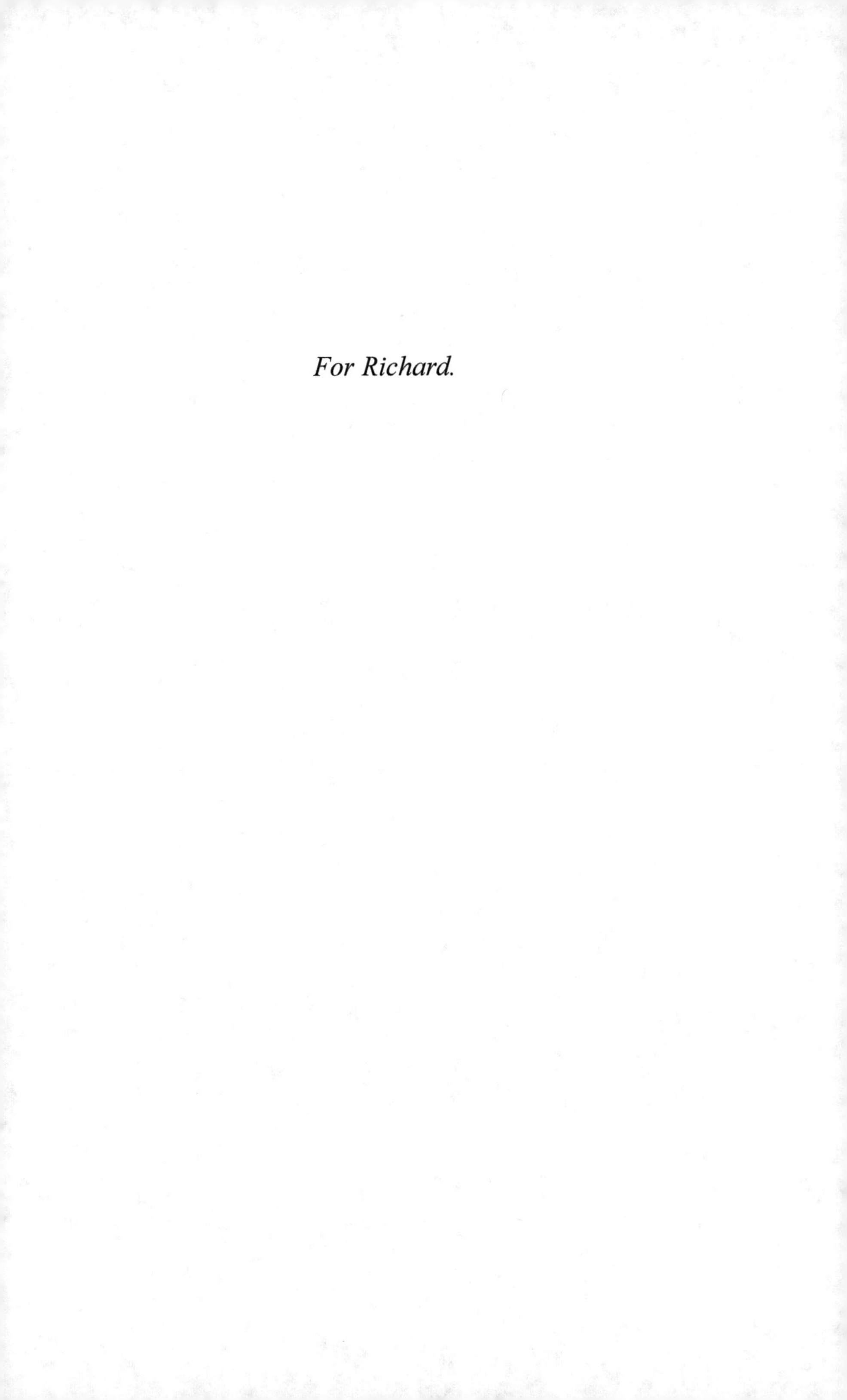

For Richard.

CHAPTER 1

It stood upright, had the spindly limbs of a young boy, and stretched one arm through the opening between bars and toward the rabbit cages. Animal noises permeated the lab's back room. There were squeals, whines, chattering, as well as moans of pain and sighs of defeat. Some animals had been stitched up. Others had limbs wrapped in a cast. Terrariums sat on benches along one wall and were occupied by lab rats, lizards of various kinds, beetles and bugs, and a variety of snakes. The cages resting on metal racks held rabbits and guinea pigs, but also exotic animals like lemurs, koala bears, sugar gliders, hedgehogs, and squirrel monkeys.

The lights were off, but the emergency EXIT light created a dim red glow in the room. Enough light to see.

The beast stretching its arm through the bars glanced around its immediate area, looking for something. What?

Four other beasts like it, but inside their own cages, appeared uninterested in this one beast's activity. Their heads drooped with the fatigue of the day behind them. They sat languid on short, built-in seats in the corner of their cages. The stench of a short toilet occupied another corner. The rest of their cages were bare except for a few multi-colored, multi-shaped rubber toys, buckets, balls. Each cage had a sign with a number on it. The farthest was Twenty-eight, then Twenty-nine, Thirty-one, and the beast stretching toward the rabbit cage was Thirty-four.

Thirty-four didn't feel languid, didn't sit quietly on his bench. He felt hungry. An immense hunger that started deep—more deeply after watching the others eat. A half hour ago, the attendant had skipped feeding Thirty-four after he had lunged toward the food being brought in a bucket. The attendant swatted at the cage with a stick, which made a loud noise when it struck the bars. When the beast wouldn't retreat to the rear of the cage, the attendant left without feeding him.

Thirty-four knew the attendant wouldn't be back with more food. So he would have to feed himself. After looking around and not finding a tool to use, Thirty-four reached through the bars again. Another inch and his fingers would touch the rabbit cage. His shoulder pinched as he tried to force himself through the bars in desperation. A painful grimace spread across his face as he slacked and pulled his arm back. In a moment of anger, he burst against the side of the cage, grabbed two bars, and shook violently, as though he could shake the cage open. Then something occurred to him. Grabbing the bars with both hands, the beast lifted one foot and rested it near his hands, then pushed his other foot through the bars, stretching his leg toward the rabbit cage. With a few toes, it gripped the cage and dragged it forward, scraping it noisily along the shelving until it landed with a loud crash onto the ground. Thirty-four jumped to the ground, knelt next to the bars, and reached through to pull the cage closer. With a broad smile cast along his wide mouth, Thirty-four opened the simple latch, reach into the cage, grabbed the rabbit, yanked it from one cage and into the other. With a simple twist of the neck, the rabbit became limp. Thirty-four bent the rabbit back to expose its soft stomach. Its backbones cracked and broke in the beast's hands. He bit into the soft fur, wrenching its head to tear the skin open. Then he pushed his fingers into the flesh and pulled, letting the guts spill to the ground. He walked to the corner of his cage and sat on the floor, blood running down his chin as he pulled and chewed at the meat.

One of the other beasts, Twenty-nine, stared, then got up and walked closer to see what was going on. Thirty-four held the limp and bloody rabbit toward the other and said, "You want some?"

The second beast shook its head. "Trouble," Twenty-nine said.

Thirty-four ignored the warning. Hunger beat out all worry. He smiled for a moment before delving back into his meal. Before he ate very much, fingers and face sticky with blood, Thirty-four felt his stomach churn in an unusually painful and uncomfortable way. He ran to the toilet and threw up. Coughed and spit, then threw up again.

Thirty-one raised his head and laughed. Thirty-four threw the rabbit carcass toward the other's cage, but the body caught on one of the cage bars and fell to the ground. Thirty-four felt even hungrier now and there was nothing to eat. He walked toward the rabbit and picked it up, looked at it, brought it close to his mouth, then threw it to the other side of the cage. Thirty-four sat in the middle of the cage and lowered his head. He sniffled.

"You crying?" Twenty-nine asked.

"No."

"His crying," Thirty-one said, then stood and walked closer. The four cages sat side by side with several feet between them so that the beasts couldn't touch.

"Don't," Thirty-one said. "Sorry I laughed. Don't cry."

Thirty-four turned away while still sitting and let the tears fall. With its back toward the others, it could imagine being alone. He was still inside a cage, but could imagine being free if he squinted and stared long enough between the bars.

CHAPTER 2

Tempest Eugene Nesbit, Ten to his friends, sat staring at the blank television screen. He had just turned it off. Three a.m. His fatigue wouldn't let him fall asleep. Memories held him in check. His wife had been murdered. She was pregnant at the time. If only he had rushed home after being laid off, he could have prevented it. And if had not been able to save her life, at least they'd both be dead. He wouldn't be sitting in front of the blank screen of a television set in the dark.

He focused his attention on his face, his eyes, and tried to will the tears to come, will himself to cry. But no tears came, which only made him feel worse about the fact that he was alive and she was dead. Dropping his head to his chest and shaking it slowly, he recalled the recent past: running from the government, the short but intimidating trials, and his eventual freedom. Ten placed his hands on top of his head, tried to bring on the tears again, but he was tear-dry. Leaning back on the couch, he let out a short laugh at himself. The sound shoved the silence violently out of the room, but only for a moment. Then everything quieted again. Life slowed. His life stopped. The whole Earth seemed to be at a standstill. Which left him completely alone. He thought he'd be able to rest once he went free, once everything was over. But instead, that's when the immense horror and tragedy of what had happened rushed in.

He let it play through his memory once again. His vengeful first murder, the second killing, his complete reversal of focus, and after all that, the eventual request, from the president himself, to join the agency that had ruined his life. The people responsible were in jail and he had been acquitted. Was it supposed to be some kind of miracle, a sentence, a cosmic joke? How the hell did everything work out the way it had?

The whole system was fucked up.

Whenever Ten allowed himself to dwell on the single fact that mattered—his life partner was gone—he wanted no part of any of it. That couldn't be a miracle. He got his revenge, but those images now haunted him as well. No matter how tired he got, sleep didn't come until exhaustion forced its hand.

In the dark, Ten walked into the kitchenette of his small apartment without bumping into anything. Once there, a lone nightlight allowed him to see well enough to extract a sleeping pill from its thin bottle and swallow it without water. The dry pill scratched his throat going down. He let his head remain back, gathering saliva and swallowing a second time to smooth its progress. He stared at the ceiling, took a deep breath, held it for seven or eight seconds, and let the air out slowly. He felt numb, anxious, responsible, cheated, and horrified, not only by what had happened but also by his part in it all. At the time, shooting a man in the face got compartmentalized in his head and shoved into a back closet. Now, in memory, he saw it all in slow motion over and over again. At first, he couldn't bring up the memory; now it wouldn't go away.

He removed a paring knife from the drawer and pulled up his t-shirt sleeve to expose his shoulder. In the dim light, dark patches of skin, like lines in the sand, showed where several scars already stretched down his arm. Some cuts still weren't fully healed. He pressed the paring knife into his skin and pulled it along until the pain registered, made him feel, made him sense something about the world. Blood oozed out of his arm as he held the knife under the spigot, turned on the cold water, and rinsed it. He splashed water over his arm too. The water stung the area, a second indication that he was still alive, that he could feel pain. He stared. But he still couldn't cry.

Nothing worked.

He held a hand towel over his punctured skin until he felt the bleeding had ended. At the refrigerator, as though nothing had just happened at all, Ten removed a bottle of apple juice and drank out of the container before putting it back. He reached over and yanked the nightlight from the socket. Everything went dark. He headed into the bedroom to undress. His head hadn't even hit the pillow when the phone rang, so he sat back up, reached for his shirt, which lay across the arm of the chair he sat in to dress and undress, and slid his vibrating cell phone from the pocket. He didn't look to see who called at this hour. "Hello."

He heard a few clicks come from the phone as though a computer was transferring the call because he picked up. Before he had the chance to drop the call, a voice said, "It's Jacob."

Ten felt instantly confused. "What do you want?"

"I could use your help. I'm really sorry, but I have no one else to turn to."

"I refused to work for ISTI even before the trials started. Why do you think I'd help now? Unless this is personal, and you need to borrow money, or my car, the answer's no."

"Hear me out…"

Ten took a deep breath, wishing the sleeping pill would kick in. He glanced at the clock. "It's 3:23. Can it wait?"

"There's a mad scientist doing some pretty awful things."

Ten looked at his arm where he'd cut himself again. He could see the mark in the glow of the phone face. "I'm finding that a lot of scientists are mad or confused as to the dangers they're putting everyone into these days. Technology, science, biology, chemistry: it's all so advanced anymore that we put ourselves in danger without even knowing it. Look at the speed of the Large Hadron Collider. Seriously, what if it *did* create a black hole."

"Jesus, Ten, how long have you been up? Anyway, it didn't happen. We're still here." Jacob sounded annoyed by Ten's tangent. "You never believed it would anyway."

"I know, but our beliefs aren't always right. Sometimes they blind us."

"It's too late for philosophy, for God's sake. Let me tell you about this problem I have."

"Go." Ten wiped his palm over his face and closed his eyes as he sat on the edge of the bed listening to his friend, who had become the chief of staff at ISTI. International Security for Technological Innovation.

"There's this group—we're trying to narrow down the main guys—playing around with animal-human hybrids. They're looking to make an army of them, we believe."

"Sounds like science fiction."

"I know, but so did that killing machine we all worked on for all those years."

"Aren't wars fought using technology these days? What the hell would you do with a hybrid army?" Ten felt a bit fuzzy. Maybe the pill was kicking in. "Besides, it would take twenty years for the damned things to mature, wouldn't it?"

"Some countries create armies from using children, you know that. Besides, there are plenty of ground troops everywhere. That's not going away."

"So what do you want from me?"

"Follow up on our findings."

"Have your own people follow up. You're in charge over there. Besides, I'm not working for ISTI."

Ten pulled the phone from his face, then heard Jacob yell through the speaker. "It's freelance!" Jacob yelled.

Ten brought the phone back to his ear. "What's that supposed to mean?"

"We've been ordered not to proceed with any heavy amount of time and support looking into the case. But it's been going on for a little over ten years. The kids, or whatever, would be about the right age. It's not viewed as a huge threat yet and we have other projects we're deep into."

"Orders," Ten said. "Maybe they're right. The big bosses. I thought you'd have more power to make those decisions, but it looks like they have you by the balls too. You appear to have limited reach and limited capability. My suggestion is to listen to your bosses. Besides, I tend to agree."

"Maria doesn't."

"What about Maria?" Ten felt responsibility, guilt, thread through his veins. "I thought Maria wasn't involved with ISTI either. After her boyfriend…"

"Whoever is doing the experiments is impregnating women with the hybrids, girls they abduct from all over the world," Jacob said.

"Her pet project."

"Exactly. Part of this is her fault. She found something out somehow, asked me to research it, then asked me to get involved. I can't do that. You know Maria and women's rights. It appears, from what little I know, that the child kidnapping trade is selling to this screwed up clan of misfit criminals so the girls can be used as surrogate mothers for the hybrids. We might be able to stop two things at once if we catch them."

"We? I don't know," Ten said, to his own surprise.

"Not *we* in the sense that you'd be working for us. You'd be independent. I can pay you out of a private fund. No one has to know." Ten didn't respond right away. He was thinking. "You can quit whenever you want. Just make the call."

"Sounds sketchy."

"It is."

"You only get one *get out of jail free* card."

"I know, Ten. I know." Jacob sounded tired, depleted, and Ten wondered about how many hours he worked. After all, it was after 3:30 by now. "We were all lucky. But this is different. Look, just talk with Maria. That's all I ask. If you still don't want to get involved, I'm good with that."

"If I'm not working for ISTI, I don't take orders, right?"

"We can help you along the way."

"But no orders."

"Right. I don't even want anyone to know that I talked with you," Jacob said. "Until I have to."

"Sounds serious. You could get into a lot of trouble, I take it."

"I could." Jacob sounded confident again, as though he pulled himself together.

"And I could get arrested."

"You could."

"And go to jail this time." Ten felt a surge of excitement rush through him and wasn't sure where it came from.

"Yes."

Chapter 3

Ten woke with a terrible headache, unsure for a moment where he was. His conversation with Jacob slowly came back to him. *Was it an actual conversation?* He checked his phone and, surprisingly enough, Jacob had called him. Of course it was real. He slapped his forehead as though knocking sense back into his head. He didn't feel so depressed that he couldn't tell reality from dream. He took a deep breath and stretched his arms when he stood. His elbows and knees cracked. His muscles felt stiff as he twisted around. He thought about the night before when he felt the pull of tight skin around his shoulder. Sometimes he wasn't sure if what he felt, or didn't feel, was depression or something else completely. What did it matter anyway? It was morning, another morning. He brushed a hand over his most recent cut.

It hardly hurt, making the event surreal in his mind.

He slugged into the bathroom, showered and dressed, then popped two Advil before opening the refrigerator to see what was available for breakfast. Yogurt. Better than nothing. He removed a spoon from the silverware drawer, peeled the barrier from the yogurt cup, and spooned some into his mouth. Each sound he made, the shower, opening the drawer and then the refrigerator, peeling the lid from the yogurt, it all broke the silence inside his apartment.

He noticed the red numbers on the microwave indicated 10:30. He had slept better than usual and felt more rested than he had in a long while. Once he stopped doing things that made noise, the apartment became too quiet, so he flipped on the radio for some classic rock background music. He and Amy used to listen to classic rock while in bed at night while they read, or while they messed around, snuggling, tickling, sometimes leading to love. He smiled at the memory, then quickly felt a deep sadness, the plunge of a roller coaster dropping into its first turn. She was beautiful, fun, kind, independent…

He plopped onto the couch with his yogurt until he finished, then set the cup and spoon on the floor near his feet. He pulled his cell phone from his shirt pocket and called Maria as Jacob had recommended.

The first thing she said was, "Jacob told me he called you."

"He called early this morning around three but didn't really give me much information. He just said to talk to you."

"I don't think he had much to offer." Maria's voice was just as he'd remembered it, soft but direct. "All I know is that young girls are being kidnapped in foreign countries, brought over here, and artificially inseminated. It's a horrible crime." She sounded upset just talking about it.

"What happens after they give birth?" Ten asked.

"I don't want to think about it. How gross and awful it must be for them. And if they knew what was inside them, how could they live with that? How could they?" She almost screamed into the phone.

He wanted more information but didn't want to upset his friend any more than she obviously was. "I never asked what they were birthing," he said as quietly and unobtrusively as possible.

"Chimpanzees."

Ten made a face and shook his head. He didn't understand. "They're birthing monkeys?"

"Not exactly. In the early 1900s, a Russian scientist, Ilya Ivanovich was his name, experimented, for the first time, with artificial insemination. At one time, he tried it with human sperm and chimps. He wanted to create stronger humans. But his experiments didn't work. They didn't take. He was about to use chimpanzee sperm with a human egg when they shut him down. He was calling them Humanzees."

"And you believe that's what they're doing? Can that be done? You'd think if it could…"

"I know that's what they're trying to do, whether they can or not... but medicine has come a long way in over a century. Even if Ivanovich couldn't do it, that doesn't mean we can't do it now with our technology. There is a chromosome imbalance, so I'd suspect the offspring would be sterile, but I can't even be positive about that. I can hope. It would provide a stopgap. The whole thing has a huge moral weight around its neck, as you can imagine. Look at the controversy around cloning humans. Crossbreeding them with chimpanzees… impossible to get through. No one could get financial backing for anything close to this kind of experiment. Imagine the outcry. It would take—"

"A foreign government," he finished her line. "But which one?" Ten sat on the edge of the couch cushion with interest. Maybe the project could be something for him to do; maybe a distraction would help. For whatever reason, the situation had hold of him for now. Maybe it was Maria's engagement, maybe he needed to sleep better. He scooped up the yogurt container and stood while holding the phone to his ear. A short walk to the kitchen and he threw the container away and dropped the spoon into the sink. He saw the knife from the night before still sitting there. He hardly remembered the incident, even though he was positive it took place. He had proof. At the moment, he felt a little ashamed and turned his head away.

"I don't really care which country is involved," she said, "and I don't care why they're doing the research, or how it all works. I want to save those girls." She paused as though waiting for a response. "We have to stop them." Her voice had lowered into something more serious.

Ten closed his eyes. Was this what he needed? Probably not. "I don't know how I can help. What about a detective? I mean there must be plenty of other people out there who are better qualified to do this."

"Moral support, first of all. You also have technology experience that I don't have." She took a short breath. "And you think differently than anyone I've ever met. You come at problems from an angle, a tangent." She waited again. "And I trust you."

"You don't trust Jacob?"

"Not like I trust you. I've seen you in action. You're not afraid. No matter how dangerous or frightening the situation, you appear to be able to just take care of things."

"I compartmentalize them," he said, knowing his own strengths and drawbacks and spelling it out in one word. What he was good at could save his life or kill him, in the long run.

"You went through hell and came out okay, better than most of us. So, whatever you do, you are able to stay calm, and that's something I feel I can rely on."

"Numb might be more like it." Ten pushed up his sleeve and rubbed his latest cut.

"I don't take you as numb," she said.

He wanted to tell her that's how he felt, whether she wanted to take it that way or not. But he didn't say any such thing. He agreed to work with her. "I can help, but only because it's you. I owe you that much."

"You don't owe me anything."

"I disagree, but that's not the issue here, is it? The issue is how do we acquire the information we need if Jacob can't be involved? And if he's not involved, if ISTI isn't involved, then how do we keep from being caught? And even if we figure all this out, then what happens to us?"

"A lot of questions."

"Any answers?"

"There are answers to every question if you look in the right places. I do have it on fairly good authority that Jacob can watch over us. He'll want whatever information we find out. He just can't allocate his people on the project at the moment. But mostly, I'm thinking of those poor girls," Maria said. Ten could hear the strain in her voice. He knew instantly she was telling the utmost truth, her deepest truth, that whatever she did, she wanted to help those girls.

"Where do we start?"

He heard some rustling of papers in the background. "I found some very interesting information at the lab where I work. Whenever I see the least thing that doesn't seem right, I get nervous. Probably because of what happened with that nanobot thing."

"We're not supposed to talk about that. Not even over the phone."

"I know. I'm sorry," she said. "The point is that while looking through paperwork, I noticed something wrong and it bothered me. I've learned to take that seriously. I have the name of a doctor and I have an address for his clinic. His wife works here, but I don't think she knows what's going on. Maybe she does, but she's a good liar. Anyway, I think that's enough to start with."

"I get the feeling that you know more than you're saying. Be that as it may, what do you want me to do? Go over to his office and ask why he's sending packages to his wife?"

"I called for your help. Maybe poke around the Internet or something. Collect information for now. We can talk more later. Like you pointed out earlier, maybe the phone isn't the best place to talk about this."

"I didn't say that."

"You insinuated it when you suggested we stay away from certain topics."

"I was just saying…"

"Ten, listen. Look up whatever you can find on a Dr. Carl Clarkson. He's done a lot of research on cloning, but also on artificial insemination. It may not be the best lead, but that's what I have for now. Then meet me this evening. I get off work around five. We can talk further then. I am so glad you said yes." She hung up.

Ten hung up the phone and instantly fell to his knees. He lowered his head against the refrigerator door. What was he thinking? Why was he willing to do this all over again? Wouldn't it be dangerous once they met the criminals involved? He was sure no foreign government was going to like having two scientists futzing around with their people. And Jacob couldn't help? But yet Maria said he could watch over them? Not everything made sense and Ten liked things to make sense. He was an engineer after all. And she never went into how she knew about the girls. What the hell?

And if they got caught? There was no way he would get out of jail a second time. The president wouldn't be able to spring him again. He doubted anyone would even try.

Chapter 4

Abdi Karimi sat behind a grand oak desk with his elbows rested on top, the fingertips of both hands touching. A Kel-Tec 9mm sat in front of him, pointing away, pointing toward two men who stood in front of him. He had not even glanced at the gun, a permanent fixture on his desk.

The two men stood, stiff and straight, their chins pointing down, their eyes averted, silent, their breathing shallow. A trickle of sweat left the hairline of one man and ran down along his cheek. He appeared not to notice.

A third man reclined in a stuffed chair, which rested against the side wall perpendicular to where Abdi held court. The third man was older than the two men, but not as old as Abdi, the eldest and most accomplished of seven brothers.

Abdi turned to the third man. "Mon," he said, "what would you do?"

"How many strikes?" Mon said in an even tone. He didn't look at Abdi or at the two men. His face exhibited the blank look of a disinterested bystander. One who hardly cared to answer the question asked of him. Bored.

Abdi stood from his chair and placed his hands near the pistol as he lifted up. The two men jerked slightly from the surprise of movement in the room after such a long silence. The one on the right, dressed in a green t-shirt and khakis, let out a small sound. Abdi looked directly at him. "I understand you didn't feed number Thirty-four." He waited for an answer.

Finally, after a long, uncomfortable pause, the man in the green shirt lifted his chin slightly. "He was aggressive. He knocked the bucket of fruit from my hands."

"You were afraid of him?" Abdi turned his head and smiled at Mon. "He's afraid of a five-year-old hybrid."

"It was a punishment," the man blurted out. "He didn't deserve the food. He had to learn."

"And you make that decision? You don't ask anyone else, like perhaps Dr. Shirazi? He's in charge at the clinic, isn't he?"

"It was a night feeding. Everyone had gone home," the green-shirted man said. The man next to him remained completely silent.

Abdi sat on the corner of his desk and placed his hands in his lap. "You," he said with some anger, "do not make such decisions. Your job is to do as you are told. You are told to feed, you feed. Now look what happened." He shook his head in disgust.

"But they're vegetarians," the man in green said in a voice so low it could hardly be heard.

"Chimpanzees?" Abdi shrugged. "Maybe most of the time, but humans, on the other hand, have been omnivorous since the beginning. And number Thirty-four has found that out. He has tasted blood." Abdi smiled at Mon, since Green Shirt continued to stare at the ground. "All because you were angry with him and decided he didn't deserve his dinner. When Dr. Shirazi checked the videos last night, he couldn't believe his eyes. The ruthlessness of the beast. He was afraid of it this morning. And the little bastard shook its cage, screamed, reached for more rabbits even though it had vomited what it had eaten. When it was fed, it shoved the bucket away. It wants meat now."

"I'm sorry," Green Shirt said. "It won't happen again."

"I know. It will never happen again. Not by you." Abdi reached for the 9mm with his left hand, brought it around, and pulled the trigger twice, pummeling two rounds into Green Shirt's chest. The other man tensed, but remained standing, becoming even more stoic if that was possible.

Green Shirt crumpled to the floor as though deflated. Blood wicked through his shirt and onto the floor, already puddling.

Abdi set the gun back down on the desk, pointed away. He stared at the other man, who appeared to be trembling slightly. "Now you. What have you got to say?"

The man swallowed and opened his mouth. It took a moment before words came. "I didn't know what happened. Busy with other duties. The video…"

"I believe that," Abdi said. "I also heard that from Shirazi, who did watch the video."

The man looked as though he were about to cry, his lower lip and chin quivered, his hands shook. Yet there was a slight sag to his shoulders, as though he felt relieved.

"Your job is to make sure the other person does their job, and their job is to make sure you do yours. That's why there are always two of you working together. No one person takes the blame for the other. You work together. It's all or nothing."

The man's shoulders slouched further and started to shake. The man looked away, toward Mon, who remained sitting near the wall. "Please," the man said through a bubble of spittle.

Abdi reached for the gun and the man lifted his arm over his face.

Abdi laughed.

The man lowered his arm slightly.

"I'm not going to shoot you. One dead is enough. You are responsible for each other, but both don't have to die." He turned to Mon. "Do they both have to die?"

Mon shrugged, but still didn't make eye contact with Abdi.

Abdi stood and took a step toward the man trembling before him. He placed the muzzle of the pistol against the man's chest. "If I pulled the trigger, you probably wouldn't die, but it would hurt and you'd remember, wouldn't you?"

The man said nothing. He swallowed hard. When the barrel of the gun pushed harder against him, he nodded.

"But there's no reason to do that." Abdi turned around and walked back to the other side of his desk. He placed the gun down. "You will select a partner to work with and you will not make this mistake again. Once we decide what to do with Thirty-four, you will handle it. Whatever we want you to do, you will do… with your new partner. Do you understand?"

"Yes, sir." As though his muscles were still locked, the man's arm jerked as it lowered back by his side. He took a larger breath than he had since arriving.

Abdi noticed every detail of the man's movements, of the man's fear. He could almost smell it, and wondered, only for a moment, why he hadn't shot this man as well. "You are dismissed."

The man stumbled when he turned around but didn't fall. His walk was uneven. He struggled with the doorknob. The man's trembling had become so bad that he didn't appear to be able to function. He closed the door behind him twice before it latched.

Abdi laughed out loud. "Did you see that? I thought he was going to shit himself." He tapped the desktop with his finger as he walked around and plopped down in the chair. "He won't disobey any of our orders now." He tapped his desktop with his knuckle to make a louder sound. "That's how you get men to take orders. To do as they're told." He stared at Mon, but Mon never turned to look at him. Mon never shifted in his chair. Abdi slammed a fist on his desk. "Did you see that?"

Mon turned slowly toward Abdi. "My friend, that is how you learned."

"Yes, it is. And that is how I train these men. A firm hand. It's been years."

"It has been that," Mon responded.

"I'm surprised these mistakes even happen anymore. Don't they talk amongst themselves? Are they stupid?" He waved a hand, not at Mon, but through the air, a gesture of dismissal or surrender. "My brothers send us new people to work with but look what we get. The worst of the worst. They are not professionals. They are farmers, stupid villagers." He leaned forward, grabbed the pistol and placed it into the top drawer to his right. "My friend, would you mind going out to find someone to clean this mess up for us?"

Mon rose from his chair and walked out the door without a struggle.

Abdi leaned back in his chair. He could see an outstretched arm and part of a shoulder with a green sleeve over the right side of his desk. The rest of the man wasn't visible. The hand and arm were twisted in an unnatural way. He shifted his chair toward the left until he couldn't see the arm. He looked up at the closed door and spoke to it as though anyone could hear him. "Hurry," he said. "I'm tired of looking at this."

He tapped the top of his desk with the fingers of his right hand. Sometimes he wondered what Mon really thought of their situation, what he thought of Abdi and his methods. All Mon ever did was tell Abdi what he already knew. He wanted Mon to notice more, respond more. His friend didn't even flinch when the man was shot.

Abdi slammed his hand on the top of the desk, then heard the door latch. Two men came in to remove the body and clean the floor. Abdi left as soon as they arrived. He needed a rest.

Chapter 5

It felt good driving over to see Maria that evening. They had both moved to Virginia, but for different reasons. Maria took a job with Mutual Consolidated Labs (MCL), one of the largest in the country. Her expertise and security clearance gained her a position of power where she headed a team of researchers. She put in long hours, but always looked satisfied with her life whenever Ten saw her.

Ten moved hoping to get away from where he used to live, to be alone in his grief, yet be around some of the people he'd shared the last year with. Since Jacob and the International Security for Technological Innovations (ISTI) were located in Virginia, he somehow felt that he had a support group, and did have one for a short while, until everyone's lives settled into their new positions.

After parking in her drive, Ten knocked on her door. Maria's curly hair and wide eyes always surprised Ten if he hadn't seen her for a while. She always looked as though the world was a wonder-filled place and she was happy to be there. He knew the torment she'd gone through, the hours of therapy, and the fear that someone was still after her. But she seemed to be over that now, especially with her willingness to work on such a project as she'd asked him to help with.

They hugged at the door to her house. "How have you been?" she asked him.

"Surviving." There wasn't much more to say. He'd basically been a shut-in for the last few months, keeping his apartment dark with the blinds down and the lights off.

"I hear you." She walked down a short hall and shot left into the kitchen. "Have a seat. Want something to eat?"

"I'm good." Ten sat at the counter on a tall stool and leaned to place an elbow on the tile top.

"You're still not working." She said it like an accusation.

"I am now," Ten said.

"Yeah, I guess you are." Her tone was buoyant. "I'm sorry to get you mixed up in this. I didn't think I'd ever want to do anything like this ever again. I had had enough. But my psychologist said that the excitement might be something I craved for a while." She reached for two glasses from a cabinet. Then went to the refrigerator and removed a bottle of Riesling.

Ten held up his hand. "I try not to drink very much anymore. It worsens my mood."

"It'll help you sleep though," she said.

"Do I look like I don't sleep?"

She leaned over the counter. "Absolutely." She poured wine into the two wine glasses and lifted hers toward him. "To a safe undertaking."

Ten had to laugh. He picked up the goblet. "Here, here." Ten clinked glasses with her and took a long swallow. "I like a good Riesling."

"You look a little nervous."

"Besides tired?"

"Yeah. You're kind of a mess. Is everything okay?"

He wanted to be honest with her. But he also wanted to retain his privacy. He couldn't do both and wasn't sure which to do. "I'm still a bit unsure if this project is the right thing for me to be doing right now."

"Me either. I'm not sure my shrink is terribly happy about it either." She shrugged. "But it's my life, I suppose. And I wouldn't be involved if it wasn't for those poor girls.

There's something about that. Not just the kidnapping, the abductions, but forcing them to carry a baby that's not human, then taking that from them too. The whole thing…"

Ten took a deep breath. He could see her concern, her anger. "So, what do you know?"

"More than I wanted to talk about over the phone. You probably guessed that."

"I did. That's why I took you up on your invitation. I can hardly be expected to make a full commitment without all the details."

"Jacob and his team actually found out about this through ISTI. They keep track of a lot of scientific things going on, not all of them ones that the government is in charge of either."

"Like our first project for that killing machine," Ten said.

"Jacob says that there are tighter controls on the people involved now though. With him in place, it's less likely that scientists are in danger."

"You mean from our own government." Ten stared at the wine as he rolled the goblet in his hand. "And you said 'less likely,' which doesn't help a lot either. But you were saying that he's been paying attention to scientific advancements even when the government isn't involved."

"Exactly." She set her glass down, took his from him, and set it down as well.

She wanted his attention, so he looked up at her.

She nodded. "They had suspicions that Clarkson was up to something pretty serious, but no real data. I happened to be at the right place at the right time."

"MCL is involved."

"Not exactly. Going through some files, I found paperwork passing through one of the employees. Well, more than just paperwork. Packages. I told you some of this, I believe."

Ten interrupted her story. "Is that really that unusual?" He reached for the glass again and stood, holding it near his chin as though ready to take a sip.

Maria raised her eyebrows and smiled. "No, packages go through MCL all the time, but these packages moved between a veterinarian's office and a doctor's office. That is unusual."

"So did you go to Jacob or did he come to you?"

"He had mentioned to me one night while having dinner that he thought MCL was somehow involved in illegal dealings. It's a big place, so I wasn't too surprised there might be individuals involved. But it was afterward that I found the paperwork and called him with my suspicions."

"So the pieces are fitting together pretty quickly." He reached toward Maria with his glass in salute.

"A toast?" she asked.

"To you and Jacob. I didn't know…"

"You still don't, Ten," she said with a shake of her head. "We have dinner once in a while, that's all. You and I did that a few times too, when we all first moved here. And you've been out with Jacob. Should I suspect something there? You're not gay, are you?"

Ten had to laugh at her anger. He wasn't sure if he had hit a nerve or she was transferring her anger about the girls, or she just didn't want to be interrupted so often. He figured he'd better back off. "No, you're right. I guess I was hoping that at least one of us, or two, was having a normal life after all this time."

She calmed quickly. "I'm sorry. We're all… well." She shrugged again. "I have talked with Roger once or twice over the phone. He appears to be moving on nicely."

"He wasn't as involved as the two of us. Neither was Jacob. You and I saw the brunt of that mess." He looked away so he didn't have to meet her eyes.

"Well, my therapist says that a more normal life is coming." She got serious for a moment. "You should go see one. The rest of us have. It's helped Jacob and Roger."

"I thought you trusted me because I can compartmentalize things."

"I do."

"I don't need to talk to anyone but you guys, thank you very much."

"It might help," she said. "You do look like you haven't slept well."

"I'm fine." He knew he sounded a bit curt, but he was finished with that particular discussion and wanted to get back to the situation at hand. "So, do we just go after this vet, the doctor, who? Is that what Jacob expects us to do? And what are we supposed to do when we catch these people? Arrest them? We can't do that."

"Everything passes through an employee at MCL. She's actually the wife of the doctor."

"That changes things, doesn't it?"

"I'll keep an eye on her. In the meantime, we collect information for Jacob. If there is another government involved, then this might be serious business—"

"If they're actually creating these hybrids," Ten said.

"Yes, then he thinks he can get ISTI to open the case, as it were."

"And he can step in."

"That's what he says."

"In the meantime, we're vigilantes."

"Something like that."

"You're not afraid you'll lose your job?"

"I'm going to save those girls." She said the words with a conviction Ten had never heard from her. He didn't ask why it was so important and wasn't about to ask. He suspected that her therapy had brought up more stuff than just what happened when their last project ended. That was another reason not to go to therapy, he thought; he didn't want to dredge up anything else. He had enough on his mind.

They discussed the case for another half hour. Maria filled him in on why it was unusual for packages to go through the lab from a veterinary facility to a human one. She touched on what she knew about children being abducted in third-world countries and why that part of it made sense. "The media talked about the abductions as though it's because of disputes, that certain factions are taking the boys for the armies. But in a few countries, there have been huge increases in female abductions. Stories abound, of course, and some of them link back to our doctors."

"Directly?"

"Indirectly. From a hospital in Iran. In fact, from our vet to the doctor to the hospital and back to the vet. Our vet works closely with the zoo."

"Apes," Ten said.

"More wine?" Maria held up the bottle.

"I think so."

Chapter 6

Thirty-four sat in the corner of his cage sulking. He ate some of the fruit from his bucket, but not all of it. He wanted meat, even though the last time he ate it he got sick. There was something about the flavor or texture. Luckily, he learned that if he was too eager to get to his bucket of food, the handler backed away and it postponed its arrival. Twenty-eight had explained it to him. When he tried it, it worked. If he sat quietly or stood to the side of his cage, the person would feed him, often first. The two who came to feed him also fed the others. The others were curious and interacted with the two feeders, so they all spent more time together. Thirty-four sulked because they ignored him.

When Donya, his trainer, came she brought him some meat that tasted different than the rabbit he had eaten. The meat was darker in color and somehow didn't cause him to retch or give him stomach pains. He looked forward to more of it for other meals. He hoped it was something they were now introducing.

From one of the other cages, one of the men pointed toward Thirty-four's cage and laughed. The beast he stood near, number Thirty-one, laughed too. Thirty-four turned his head to look away from them. He felt pangs of something in his chest and tears formed in his eyes. He couldn't hear what they were saying but wished he could. He wiped the tears away using the back of his hand and sat on his bench listening to the laughter; then something gripped him, ran up his spine, and exploded in his head. All his muscles tensed and, bending to some invisible drive, reacted by leaping from his corner and running toward them, only able to travel a few feet before reaching for the bars, gripping them firmly and shaking with all his might. He screamed a loud "Aaaah!" shaking his head to scare them. Both the man and the beast jerked away and Thirty-four felt justified. He raised his chin into the air and shook his head again. He knew that Donya liked it when he talked but felt defiant when he refused to. Noises felt more natural to him for some reason. After his outburst, other animals in the lab began to make noise and become active. More cages rattled. Chimps in the rear of the building chattered. Some animals yipped and others hissed. "Assholes," he said, before sitting back down.

"Who you calling an asshole, you stupid son of a bitch?" The man walked from Thirty-one's side and reached for his stick. The other man, who had been standing near a bench all this time, walked toward Thirty-four too. "Don't do anything, Safa. We'll both be in trouble. I don't want either one of us killed," Rahim said.

Donya yelled at Safa as well, just saying, "Don't."

"Okay, Rahim, but the next time…" Safa raised the stick and shook it.

Thirty-four stared at him, daring him, but Safa didn't get any closer.

Rahim placed a hand on Safa's shoulder. "Seriously, the idiot isn't worth it."

Thirty-four's anger depleted quickly, and he wandered toward the rear of his cage. The men were so much bigger than he was, but he felt stronger, more threatening. After all, they needed the stick to protect themselves. When he turned around, the men left. He sat down again. From farther down the line of cages, Thirty-one pointed at him. "No, no, no, no, no." He waved his finger as he spoke. "You did a bad. Safa will hit you."

Donya didn't appear to be interested in their conversation. She worked at some project at one of the lab tables.

Thirty-four gave his head a shake as though giving Thirty-one an adamant no. He raised his chin and pointed to himself. "I hit."

Thirty-one waved a hand at Thirty-four and walked to the far side of his cage to talk with the others. Thirty-four could see them, but not hear them except when they laughed. His anger had been spent on Safa. He sat in the middle of his cage and lowered his head. The others ignored him. Then Donya left without saying anything to him.

It wasn't until late in the afternoon when Donya returned with the other trainers. Thirty-four perked up. He had difficulty learning anything and often couldn't remember what he'd learned the day before, but he enjoyed Donya's attention. She never said anything bad to him when he failed, although she often had a look of disappointment on her face. One time, Thirty-four heard her tell the other trainers that they were lucky for getting such progress and it hurt his feelings. He tried very hard to guess colors and shapes, to say words he hadn't heard before or had heard but didn't remember.

Near the end of the session, Thirty-four said, "Safa hit," and then he touched his chest.

"He hit you?" Donya asked. "Was that during your lunch feeding, because he didn't hit you in the morning. I was here."

Thirty-four touched his chest again. "Safa hit." Then he pounded his chest.

Donya reached toward him and rubbed her hand across the fur of his arm. "I'm so sorry. I'll let someone know. I don't care how stupid you are, they shouldn't punish you."

Thirty-four cocked his head and squinted his eyes at her. "Not stupid," he said.

"No. No. I didn't mean that." She looked away, toward one of the other trainers who shook her head.

"Be careful over there," the other girl said. "You know what happened."

Thirty-four had seldom been touched and most often with the stick poking at him. The feel of Donya's hand on his arm was pleasurable. When she started to pull away, Thirty-four grabbed her wrist and pulled her closer.

She struggled and tried to pull her arm away. "Stop it!" she yelled at him.

"Not stupid," he said because he couldn't think of anything else to say at the moment. While holding her wrist, Thirty-four ran her hand over his arm again. He nodded his head as he did it, hoping she'd see what he wanted her to do, but she only struggled more, which made him angry. He pushed his face close to hers and showed his teeth. "Noooooo." In a moment, one of the other trainers he didn't even notice poked him in the ribs with one of the sticks. He heard a buzz, smelled his own hair burning, and fell to the ground in pain.

They had used the stick on him before, but usually he saw it coming. The sudden attack surprised him and the pain felt even worse. He looked up at Donya, questioning why she would let that happen. She stood above him, rubbing her wrist with her other hand. She didn't look happy. Two other trainers stood near her, one rubbed her shoulders, which made Thirty-four angry, even though he didn't know why.

"We have to report this," she said.

"If you report it, Abdi will punish someone. He'll blame us," one of the other trainers said. "Maybe we should keep it quiet. You know what happened to Ghaffar. Abdi shot him for not feeding Thirty-four."

Thirty-four wasn't sure what they talked about. What was a report? He still lay on his cage floor, wondering how long he'd be like that. Slowly, he began to gain control and sat up with some difficulty. He stared at Donya, who looked over at him once in a while as she talked with the other trainer. He wanted her to rub his arm again but knew better than to reach for her. He lowered his head and scooted across the floor toward one of the cage walls where he leaned against the bars.

"He's sulking," Donya said.

"He didn't mean anything," the girl said.

"You may be right. I'll think about it." It was early for them to quit, but Donya announced that she was leaving. "I'm still shaken," she explained.

Thirty-four didn't want her to go. He felt sorry but didn't know what to do or say. Words did not come easily to him and his actions were met with pain. He wasn't sure what to do, but to sit quietly. "Don't," he said to stop Donya from leaving, but she didn't stop, she continued to walk through the back entrance.

Twenty-eight, standing next to one of the other trainers, said, "See what you did."

Thirty-four looked around the room. He didn't know what Twenty-eight meant, but he didn't like it.

CHAPTER 7

Ten cut his arm again that evening after he returned home. Not right away. He sat in the dark for a half hour first. It was a small cut. The knife dragged across his skin a little and, for a moment, he wondered if he should choose the sharper of the paring knives to use all the time. He bled for a very short while, a dark streak appearing in the dim light. The cut was high, near his shoulder. He was still able to cover it, along with the others, with his shirtsleeve.

An hour later, he wasn't sure why he'd done it and decided it was because he was scared. Scared of his life. Scared of living when Amy was dead. And his unborn daughter. It haunted him that, had he gone home that afternoon, he could have saved her or died with her—such thoughts he allowed in over and over again.

He grabbed a handful of peanuts and a banana for dinner. He couldn't remember what he had for lunch. It didn't matter. He felt like he'd eaten enough that day. He wasn't hungry. The wine he had with Maria had given him a buzz for a short while, but that was over now.

To keep busy, he walked into his spare bedroom and opened his laptop. He began poking around about Ilya Ivanovich and found several entries in a variety of places. Ten read about the man and his plans. It didn't take long before he found a bunch of videos and documentaries about him. Some programs, some scientists, believed hybrids couldn't be created and others believed they could. No proof though. After Ivanovich, no one seemed to be studying or attempting similar experiments. Not that Ten could find anyway.

Until now.

Dr. Carl Clarkson's name was easy to find too. Worked a lot with cloning, but not just cloning, he also used different animals to gestate other animals. He tried putting the fertilized eggs of a mouse inside a squirrel, that sort of thing. It was all rather creepy to read about. Most of his experiments didn't work, but some did, and he appeared to feel as though he was getting somewhere. He was always experimenting outside his range, it appeared to Ten. Nonetheless, the guy had made a name for himself. Plus, he remained a practitioner, not just a laboratory man. He actually saw patients twice a week in a small office in a strip mall near where Ten took Taekwondo lessons, which he hadn't been to for several weeks. Maybe it was time to go back.

In a fit of interest, Ten also tapped into ISTI's database. The firewall was fairly easy to get through using a few tricks he'd learned from Roger Foramo, not that he couldn't have done it himself, but Roger was the perfect assistant and teacher at one time, and much more proficient. Ten made a note to give Roger a call sometime. Maria had said that he was adapting better than any of them. But for now, Ten opened and downloaded a case file on Dr. Clarkson to print out and read later. Then he'd have to burn it to get rid of any evidence that he was inside the ISTI database.

By the time he finished up and wandered into his living room to watch some late-night television it was already close to two in the morning. Late night was over. He flicked on the TV and went to sit down when someone knocked on his door. "Who the hell?"

"I heard that," Maria's voice came through the locked apartment door.

He rushed over and unlocked it to let her in. She stood to the side when he opened the door. "Why are you here? Do you realize—"

"I was worried."

"Worried? Maybe you shouldn't be doing this then. Either that or don't worry."

She quickly reached toward the sleeve of his t-shirt, even before she came inside.

He jumped back for a moment. "What are you doing?"

She stepped inside and grabbed his arm and pushed up his sleeve. "What's this about?"

Ten wiggled from her grasp and wrinkled his face at her. "None of your business. An accident." He couldn't think of anything. He didn't own a cat that would have scratched him. So that's all he said. "An accident."

"Several, I see. And a few of them recent."

Ten stared at her. "What do you want me to say?" He turned around and walked into the room. She followed.

"Nothing," she said.

When he turned around, she wore a sad look on her face. "Don't look at me that way. It's none of your business. I'm fine." He started for the kitchen, then stopped. When he turned around again, Maria was locking the door. "You staying?"

She looked at him and blinked. "For a long time, I blamed myself for Ben's death. I blamed myself for ever getting involved with him. But I couldn't have changed anything. There was nothing I could do, and I know that now. Ten, you're not responsible."

He wrinkled his face and closed his eyes. "I could have been there. I chose to go to the gym, to the bar."

"You weren't responsible, and you couldn't have been. Nothing can change what happened anyway. The past is over. Please… I want you to see someone."

"How did you know? I'm careful."

Maria walked closer to him but didn't touch him. She just stood there as though assessing the situation, how much she should say to him. "You can't hide things like that. I noticed a while ago but couldn't be sure." She laughed for a second. "You tend to push your sleeves up when you're talking about something that excites you. Like this case. At my house earlier, you pushed your sleeve up for a moment, then pulled it back down. I saw something but wasn't sure what it was until I did some research. This happens sometimes when people go through depression, trauma, self-doubt…"

"I don't know if I'm ready to see someone. I don't know what I'd say. I know what my problem is and I'm not willing to let it go yet. That much I know."

"Nothing. You don't have to say anything about this. It's their job to get you to where you need to go. If that means sitting quietly together, passing back and forth pleasantries, then that's what they'll do." She reached out and grabbed him by the shoulders, then let one of her hands cup his neck. "That's what my therapist said to me one of those first meetings." She shook her head. "I'm still going and it's helping." She lowered her chin and raised her eyes. "Say you'll go?"

"I'll think about it. That's all you get. So is that the only reason you came over?"

She let go of him and wandered over to the couch and sat down, looking up at him. "Pretty much. I couldn't sleep, thinking about you over here doing that to yourself. I had to face you."

"Something your therapist suggested?"

"Kind of."

"Want to stay for coffee? While you're here."

"Decaf? Is the conversation over?"

"I might be able to find some decaf. And yes, it's over. Please."

"Then I'll drink a cup with you. Then we both need to get some sleep." She followed Ten into the kitchen, where he turned on a light. "So, you been researching?" she asked.

"Yeah, downloaded a bunch of stuff, got freaked out about that Ivonovich guy, but not as much as about Dr. Clarkson. He's some kind of mad scientist. A creepy dude." Ten prepared the coffee pot and started it. He leaned against the counter.

"You don't seem depressed when we're together. I noticed that earlier when you were over."

"Don't analyze me. Anyway, I thought that conversation was over."

"You suggested that, not me," she said. "Carol Olmstead. That's my therapist. You'd like her. She's just your type. Not that I know a lot about your type, but she's smart, capable, and calm. A lot like you."

"I said maybe."

"Okay, okay." She raised her hands. Then she opened one of his cabinets, looked inside before closing it again, and opening another one. "Oh, here we go." She pulled two coffee cups from the shelf and set them next to where Ten was leaning." The coffee pot sputtered and spat near the end of its cycle.

"Make yourself at home," Ten said.

"I plan to." She opened the refrigerator and removed creamer from the door. She poured creamer into both cups. "Another name for you. Afshan Shirazi. That's the vet. Runs the Exotic Animal Clinic. I think you'll find him just as creepy as the others."

"I don't even like the sounds of his place. But that must be where they get the chimpanzees for all of Clarkson's weird science experiments. I don't even want to know how they extract the sperm."

"Don't be gross."

"Just saying." Ten swung around and grabbed the pot. He held it and asked. "What's next, now that I have information?"

"Tomorrow, either one or both of us should pay a visit to both of their offices."

"My plan exactly," he said.

"I'm going to take some time off work, so I'm going with you." She stepped out of his way.

He poured the coffee. They both grabbed a cup and walked into the living room and sat on the couch together, one at either end.

"Even decaf has a little caffeine in it. Which should keep me awake long enough to get home. What time do you want to start tomorrow?"

"Dr. Clarkson's office is near where I go for Taekwondo, so let's start there. I'll check in with my instructor too. He'll be glad to see me again. It's been weeks."

"I don't like the way you hole up here either." She raised her cup toward him. "Something else you can talk with Carol about."

"Well, you're getting me out of my apartment now."

"Only trying to help," she said.

"We'll start at 10:30. I'll pick you up."

CHAPTER 8

Even though Safa parked out back, Rahim walked around to the front of the building, went through the main entrance, and met with Dr. Shirazi at the front desk instead of going through the rear door directly into the lab and kennel area. The delivery felt important to him and the front door felt more appropriate. Besides, Dr. Shirazi would not be able to respond angrily if Rahim came to the front.

Dr. Shirazi looked up when Rahim entered and motioned for them to meet at the end of the counter where they couldn't be heard. Rahim handed the doctor the note Mon gave him to deliver. He knew what the note said and he couldn't stop his hand from shaking when he handed it over to Dr. Shirazi.

The doctor opened the paper and read the note then passed it back to Rahim. In a whisper, he said, "I don't like this. I didn't sign up for it. The beast is only a child. How could it know what it was doing?"

Rahim watched Dr. Shirazi tear the note up and throw it into the trash. What could he say to the doctor? It wasn't either of their decisions. And it wasn't just Dr. Shirazi he thought about. He could only imagine what Donya would say about the decision, after working with Thirty-four the whole time. Rahim couldn't stand the silence between them and whispered, "Abdi shot Ghaffar. Right in front of me. I have no choice but to listen. If I want to go home to my family…"

Dr. Shirazi put his hand on Rahim's shoulder and looked him in the eye. "I have to go to the zoo later today. There's a zebra…" He shook his head.

Rahim noticed only two people in the clinic's waiting area. They sat talking to each other, paying no attention to anything else. The attendant was busy typing on her computer.

"But you don't care about what I'm doing later." Dr. Shirazi motioned for Rahim to follow him into his office down the hall from the reception area. Inside, he closed the door. "Thirty-four is a child."

"I know, but you don't train them and you don't deal with them like we do," Rahim said. "You hardly go near them. He's dangerous." He lowered his eyes. "I don't like it either." He wanted to convince Dr. Shirazi, as well as himself, that it was all right, that it was the right thing to do. He said, "You must have heard that it grabbed Donya and wouldn't let her go. Someone had to tase it."

"I heard the story. It's not unusual for a child to do something like that. They're left alone, without their mothers. The trainers are all they have. They are treated like monsters. He probably wanted nothing more than her attention. She became scared without provocation. He didn't hurt her." The doctor walked to a cabinet standing against the wall of the office and removed a small bottle. Holding it in his closed hand, he turned and said, "But it is not my decision." He then pulled a syringe from his desk, unwrapped it, and removed the safety tip. He filled the needle, returned the tip, and handed it to Rahim. "Inject this into his shoulder. It'll take care of the job in less than three minutes." He turned away. "I'm sorry."

Rahim shook his head even though he held tightly to the syringe. "You have to do this. It's what you do. You're the doctor."

Dr. Shirazi stiffened at Rahim's outburst and held his hand out to stop him. "It is not my job." His look was defiant. Rahim knew that the doctor wasn't going to budge on his decision. "I can't. My job is to keep animals alive, not kill them. And at this stage, I don't believe Thirty-four is an animal. I won't have his death on my hands." He smiled an awkward grin. "And I told you, there's a zebra I have to attend to, probably be at the zoo most of the night. Again, I am sorry, but you'll have to do this."

"Don't make me," Rahim said.

Dr. Shirazi shook his head. "I will not do it. You can tell Mr. Karimi if you'd like, but what I do here is much more important than what you do. Who do you think he'll want to keep around? Just do it late at night when you can dispose of the body without my staff around or with customers coming and going." The doctor pointed to the door. "You may leave now."

Rahim's hand still shook as he placed the syringe into his shirt pocket.

"And use the rear door to the building from now on. You can buzz me from back there if you have to talk with me. But I don't want you coming through the front. None of you."

Rahim nodded and left the office, then walked through the back area past several other rooms and into a large kennel area where cages lined the walls and a row of them ran down the center. About half were filled. Few of the animals inside stirred as he walked through. A few strange looking animals moved to the fronts of their cages and others moved to the back, but most stayed where they were. The pungent odor accosted his nose and he put his arm across his face as he wound his way toward another door that led to the main lab. He walked into the laboratory where Thirty-four and the other three beasts stared at him as he sidestepped around one of the benches. He put his hand to his shirt pocket and touched the length of the syringe. He tried to avoid eye contact with any of the beasts but couldn't help looking at Thirty-four.

"Wha," Thirty-four said. His face looked childlike, innocent, regardless of the hair, thick brow, and slightly protruding jaw line.

"It's *what*, you idiot." Rahim felt sorry he'd called the thing an idiot, but it was the slowest learner. Even the others ignored it much of the time. They all knew Thirty-four was stupid.

He continued making his way through the lab toward the back where he entered the exit code on the security keypad and left the building. He stopped and closed his eyes as soon as he got outside. After a deep breath, and the feel of a cool breeze across his face, he opened his eyes and leaned his head back to glance toward the treetops and into the sky. The world was vast and wonderful, and lately he'd wondered how he had gotten himself mixed up in such a terrifying predicament. He thought he was going to help his country, but he'd done nothing so far than raise half-humans to the age of seven just to have them sent back to Iran for military training.

Rahim walked around the building and spotted the van where Safa waited for him. When he got there, Safa was standing outside smoking a cigarette. "Is it done?" Safa asked.

Rahim patted the syringe in his shirt pocket. "We have to do it later."

"I thought Afshan was to do it right away?" Safa questioned. "Why is he waiting?"

"He won't do it. We have to; tonight when we can bring the body out the back door without being seen."

"What will we do with it? You can't throw something like that into a ditch."

"Mon gave me directions to deliver it to a place that cremates animals. Someone will be there whenever we let them know we're coming. I have the information."

"You don't look happy, my friend."

"I'm not. I thought we were to deliver the body, not kill the boy."

"Don't say that. Don't call it a boy. It's a beast of some kind, but it's no boy. None of them are. Thinking that way will only make it worse."

"I don't want to do it. I do this for my family. I have been here three years. I just want to go home."

Safa took a drag from his cigarette. "Those things scare me. I'll be glad to have one of them dead… especially Thirty-four. He's mean."

"I don't want to kill anything," Rahim said, "but I don't want to die either. So, I do what I'm told."

Safa held out his cigarette.

Rahim took a long drag and handed it back.

They passed the cigarette back and forth silently until it was gone. Safa threw it on the ground and crushed the embers with the toe of his shoe.

They got into the van and pulled out of the lot. The morning was over, and midmorning brought a day of sun and warmth. The streets at that time of day had fewer travelers and, with the windows down, Rahim almost felt free. He could almost let his mind forget about what they would have to do later that evening. He thought of his wife and young boys, then about the deed he was about to perform. He couldn't get it out of his head.

Chapter 9

Maria picked Ten up at 10:30 just as she said. She drove her navy blue Camry, which she kept spotless on the outside and clean on the inside.

"I almost don't want to sit down," Ten said while climbing into the passenger seat and placing his backpack between his legs.

"Sit lightly," she said with a smile. "I've turned into a neat freak lately. It could be worse." She reached into her blouse pocket and handed him a card. "Here."

"What's this?" he asked while examining it.

"Carol Olmstead's card. You're going to go see her. I don't want my friend hurting himself."

"I'm not," Ten said as he pulled his seatbelt on.

"You're not hurting yourself or you're not my friend?"

"You're a bit too perky in the morning, you know. Neither of us got much sleep."

"I slept pretty soundly," she said.

"Well, anyway, I told you I'd think about going to see your doctor friend and that's what I'm going to do." He moved to hand the card back to her.

"I don't want you thinking about it. I want you deciding and then doing. For me. Seriously, Ten, you've been through a lot. I've read about this." She pointed across his body toward his arm where she'd seen the scars.

"So you've read about it. So have I. There are a lot of possibilities. None of them have to be correct. Besides, if you read about it, then you know it's up to me to stop it. That there are ways to make it less likely."

"I don't care about the possibilities. And I don't care about what you can do if you choose to. If you've researched it, then you also know you have a problem. I honestly don't give a shit what the problem is as long as it stops." She reached over and put her hand on his knee. "You have to." Her eyes were narrowed and her brow furrowed. She hoped that he heard her loud and clear, even if he wasn't sure what he was going to do about it. She did notice that he placed the card into his shirt pocket.

"I'll keep it until I decide," he said.

She placed the car in gear and pulled into the street. "As long as you decide to see her," Maria said under her breath.

Ten watched out the window and witnessed a short-lived bird fight, or foreplay, and then watched them take off in opposite directions. The morning air felt cool coming through the partially open window, and the sky had few clouds, letting the sunshine into the car. "First stop?" He maneuvered his backpack to a more comfortable position between his legs.

"You can put that in the back if you want," Maria said. "It'll be a lot more comfortable without it taking up all that space."

"This is fine." He patted it.

"You have a gun in there?"

He turned to look toward her in surprise. "Odd question."

"Not for this situation. We don't know what we're getting into and I know you. At least, I thought I knew you, until I realized—"

"You don't have to bring it up again." He was curt with her as he had been before.

She knew he didn't like her always bringing it up. But he was cutting himself. And from what she could tell, it wasn't just a few times. She wasn't about to let it drop.

He faced the open window as she drove. His hair blew around in the wind. He seemed angry. Hopefully, though, he also understood that she cared about his well-being. After all, she and Jacob had both helped him a lot when he first moved to Virginia. He shouldn't think they were going to stop just because he wanted them to—if he even wanted them to. It could be a cry that it wasn't over for him.

Out of the blue, he said, "I'm sorry. I just don't want to talk about that right now."

She didn't take her eyes off the road. "I understand. To answer your earlier question, about where we're going; we're going to the Exotic Animal Clinic."

"I was afraid you were going to say that. Can't we go see Dr. Clarkson first?"

"I'm driving, so I get to decide."

Ten nodded but didn't answer. They stopped for a cup of coffee on the way and had finished them before pulling into the parking lot. "That's a huge building for a veterinary hospital, isn't it?"

"It's a clinic, and he works with the zoo. He needs lots of room. Plus, there's a huge kennel of sorts, as well as the lab, which is where the packages are going in and out of. Who knows what's going on in there?"

"I think we know," Ten said.

"Well, we're here to find out." She got out of the car and came around as he was climbing out, holding onto his backpack. "Really, you're taking that now? It's a clinic. I doubt there are bodyguards or any danger. You won't need your gun. This is reconnaissance, remember? We're gathering information."

"We already know who the enemy is."

"No, we don't. Any one of these men could be in danger of their own lives and just doing what they're told. Or they could be legitimate scientists just trying to maintain some progress on their experiments. Regardless of all that, though, you have to trust me; you won't need a weapon."

Ten rolled the backpack back onto the floor of the Camry. "This time."

Maria led the way and asked for Dr. Shirazi at the front counter as soon as they walked in. The receptionist didn't even look at her computer when she told Maria that Dr. Shirazi was busy with a patient. Ten leaned forward as though he was about to say something when Maria stopped him by speaking out first. "My assistant," she said to the receptionist as she opened her purse and removed her badge from work, "and I are here from Mutual Consolidated Labs and I'm sure he's going to want to see me… us." She held out her ID for the girl to look at.

"I'll try again, ma'am."

"You'll try him the first time," Maria said, not letting the woman off the hook.

The young, dark-haired receptionist left the desk and walked into the back where she disappeared around a corner. When she came back out, she walked to the side of the counter and opened a partition for them to walk through. "He's in the second office to the left." She pointed to where they'd seen her disappear before.

"Nice work," Ten whispered.

"I got us in, now it's your turn." She knew he wasn't prepared to interrogate anyone and hoped that needing to would keep him on his toes for a while. Ten seemed pretty antsy to her and she didn't need him getting all aggressive right off the bat.

They were met at the door of Dr. Shirazi's office by a man of slight stature with a mop of very dark hair. He had bushy eyebrows and brown eyes and wore a lab coat with what looked like blood stains on it—which made sense. He welcomed them inside and to take a seat, then closed the door behind them and stepped behind his desk and sat down. With his hands visible, elbows on his desktop, and fingers clasped, he said, "How may I help you?" He looked at Maria.

Ten leaned forward and Dr. Shirazi's gaze shifted. "We're here to talk with you about the hybrids."

The doctor looked very cool and asked, "What are you talking about?"

"The Humanzees," Ten said.

A smile came over Dr. Shirazi's face.

Maria wondered if Ten's aggressive manner had actually worked. Had he gotten in already? But then Shirazi's demeanor changed and she realized the answer was no.

"You must be playing a joke," Shirazi said.

Ten tapped on the doctor's desk. "You have, or know about, hybrids being developed and, I believe shipped, if I can use that term, from your laboratory here."

Dr. Shirazi became flushed. "You have wasted my time enough." He turned his gaze back to Maria. "And you, where did you get your ID from? Who made it for you? You're not from MCL, are you?"

"I am from MCL." She glared at him for a moment, hoping he'd wonder what their visit was really about.

"Then what do you want? Be serious. I have to get back to work and I'm going to the zoo to work this afternoon. I don't have time for games."

She felt he showed more anger than what was called for. Something was up. "We'd like to take a quick walk through your facilities if you don't mind. Maybe we could see for ourselves what is going on here?"

"No, you may not. This building is for research and for caring for sick animals. It is more dangerous than you might think. You could easily make a mess of something without even knowing it. No. I don't like how you snuck in here. And I don't want you to stay. You may go now." He stood from his desk and immediately walked around toward them.

Ten and Maria stood as well. Ten was at least eight inches taller than Dr. Shirazi and Maria noticed him stretching his height as far as it would go, forcing Dr. Shirazi to look up at him.

"You can't intimidate me," the doctor said.

"I wasn't trying to."

"Just leave." Shirazi stood his ground.

Maria walked out first with Ten close behind. She noticed that he left the door open as they walked down the hall. The small agitation was done on purpose. Ten wanted to annoy the doctor, but she wasn't quite sure why. Was it to show his power or to make the doctor nervous and unsure? In a moment, the door slammed.

"He really wanted us out."

Maria nodded to Ten. As they walked out the front, Maria thanked the receptionist with a smile and a pleasant voice. When they were outside, she said, "Wow, is he ever hiding something." She turned toward Ten. "Did you notice the security system?"

"No. Was I supposed to?"

She shook her head. "That's why you're along. Not only that, but you have to get us inside that place. We've got to see what he's up to. You are the electronics genius, aren't you?"

"No one ever said that."

"Well, I am."

"I suppose you want to come back tonight for this little inspection of yours? They probably have cameras all over." He mumbled something else she didn't hear, then said, "I'll try to locate the cameras as we leave. Can we drive around the building before heading out?"

"You bet," she said.

CHAPTER 10

After failing to find Dr. Clarkson in his office that afternoon, Maria and Ten went their separate ways to prepare for the evening when they planned to regroup and break into the Exotic Animal Clinic. The temperature dropped fast after the sun went down. Ten picked up takeout Thai and ate while sitting on his couch watching the Discovery Channel.

Around eleven that night, Maria picked him up for the second time that day and drove past the Exotic Animal Clinic where she parked several blocks away. Ten brought a small drill; a multimeter; a folded pack of tools with screwdrivers, wire cutters, and needle-nose pliers; and a few diagrams he'd found online for the clinic's security system and building wiring. He'd studied the diagrams thoroughly but folded them and stuffed them into his pocket just in case. He hoped the break-in would be much easier than he anticipated. The tools were just for backup. He had stuffed everything into his backpack along with a camera, a flashlight, and his Glock 19. He figured he was ready for pretty much anything that might happen.

He and Maria walked casually along the road until they came to the clinic's main parking lot, then they raised the hoods on their sweatshirts and skirted the lot. They both wore baggy clothes to remove as much gender recognition as they could. Ten maneuvered around the lot with a laser pointer to temporarily disable the cameras, but before walking farther around the parking lot, he raised his arm, dropped his hood, and listened. He turned quickly. "A car!" Ten grabbed Maria's arm and ran with her behind a short hedge that encircled most of the lot. Bent over so they were not seen, the two of them rushed along the back of the hedge, watching a dark green van back up near the rear door, just where they were headed.

"What's going on?" Maria whispered.

"Got me. Unless they have a security crew come in every few hours or something. Makes no sense, though, with all the cameras." Ten thought for a moment. "Maybe they're here to pick something up. They did back to the door."

"Or deliver something," she said.

"Could be that too, but we'll find out in a minute for sure." Ten relaxed and sat on the ground and motioned for Maria to do the same.

She shook her head. "I need to be ready to run if I have to."

Two men got out of the van and walked toward the rear, where they opened the back doors.

"Yep," Maria whispered, "delivery."

"Hold on." Ten placed a hand on her arm. He peered through the shrub and reached out to part some branches for a better look. A cool breeze passed through the area and he saw Maria shiver for a second. "You okay?"

"Chilly is all. I'll be fine."

One of the men reached for the pin pad of the security system.

Maria pulled a small pair of binoculars from the small bag she brought with her.

Ten watched her raise them to her eyes. "Great idea."

"I have my talents too." She waved a hand at him. "Remember this: six, three, three, seven, two, five. That's the code to get inside."

"Got it." Ten half crawled farther along the hedge to get a better vantage point on the door of the lab and the rear of the van.

Rahim opened the door slowly and walked inside, Safa right behind him. They didn't turn on a light until the outside door was closed, and then only turned on one bank of lights. There was no reason to upset or awaken the animals if they didn't have to. Although a few animals stirred and some cages banged for a moment, everything settled down quickly. From the wall, Rahim grabbed a taser stick, basically a cattle prod. He handed it to Safa.

"Why me?" Safa protested.

Rahim removed the syringe from his pocket and held it up. "Would you rather go into the cage with this?"

Safa's face paled and he shook his head. He held up the taser. "I'm good."

"I thought so." Rahim walked through the back of the building, near the lab benches.

"Aren't you afraid?"

"Yes, but I want to be sure this is done right. If there's a mistake, Mr. Karimi won't be happy. And you know what I told you about that."

"You live from your fear," Safa said.

"I want to see my family again," Rahim said. He couldn't imagine not seeing his family again. If that meant living from fear, then he was fine with that. It also meant getting home. It also meant seeing his children again. He took a breath and said, "Let's get this over with."

The light allowed them to see the four cages that held the hybrid Humanzees. Thirty-four was the closest to the door, which somehow gave Rahim a better feeling. Not that it mattered, but at least he wouldn't have to drag or carry Thirty-four across the floor in front of the other three. Already he couldn't look any of them in the eyes.

All four of the beasts stirred and stood as Rahim and Safa walked toward Thirty-four's cage. Thirty-four backed into a rear corner and stared at the taser all the time Safa walked around and toward him. He edged farther along the back as Safa got closer.

"Stand still," Rahim said. He stood at the front of the cage with the key to its lock, waiting for Safa to tase Thirty-four. His palms were sweaty, and his heart pumped fast. He didn't want to go into the cage, but he didn't want to get shot by Abdi either. And he really didn't feel well, killing the boy Humanzee. He tried his best not to look at him at all. Not directly anyway. The whole thing sickened him. But he had his orders and he would follow them.

Safa edged around and toward Thirty-four too slowly for Rahim. "Hurry," he said, "we need to get this done."

Safa glared at his partner. He whispered, "He won't stop moving away from me. What do you want me to do?"

"Just be quick about it."

Then Safa rushed a few steps closer and thrust the taser end toward Thirty-four, which leaped out of the way.

"You fucking idiot," Rahim yelled at the beast.

"Asshole," Thirty-four responded.

Rahim heard Twenty-nine or Twenty-eight gasp at Thirty-four's rebuttal but ignored them. It was getting personal. He knew they understood what was going on, but wasn't aware of how much they understood, how deeply. At the moment, he didn't care. All he wanted was to get this over with, get on with his life, and perhaps end his time with Abdi. As a last-ditch effort, Rahim pointed a finger at Thirty-four. "Stay, dammit, stay!"

Thirty-four hesitated for a moment and Safa lunged the taser through the bars after rushing over to where the beast stopped. Thirty-four went down with a moan and a thud. The smell of burned fur burst into the air and assaulted Rahim's nose. Safa jumped back with a gasp. Thirty-four farted and pissed a little as Rahim unlocked the cage and rushed in to give him the shot. Kneeling near the beast, Rahim shoved the needle into the fleshy part of Thirty-four's shoulder, pushed in the poison, and removed the needle.

Thirty-four clawed at Rahim, who tried to jump back from the thrashing beast. Rahim stumbled back, then reached forward to correct himself. Thirty-four grabbed Rahim's forearm, dragged it toward his face, and bit into his arm.

Rahim hit the boy Humanzee in the chest and Thirty-four, still shaking from being tased, let him go. But Rahim didn't stop hitting the boy. Before long, Thirty-four lay quietly on the floor of the cage. Rahim's arm hurt terribly, and blood spotted his shirt. Then he noticed that his other hand had landed in a urine puddle. He screwed up his face, wiped his urine-soaked hand on Thirty-four's furry body, then stood. "That was horrible," he said with disgust. He reached for the place on his forearm where he'd been bitten but changed his mind. He didn't want to touch an open cut with his urine-soaked hand.

"Now what?" Safa asked from the cage door.

"We get him out of here," Rahim said with a snide look on his face. He thought Safa asked the dumbest questions. He turned around and noticed that the other three Humanzees were at the farthest walls of their cages, each one turned halfway around, as though that stopped Rahim and Safa from seeing them. They acted like stupid children as far as he was concerned. For a brief moment, he wondered what they thought, then let the concern slip away. What did it matter?

Safa helped Rahim by dragging Thirty-four by the legs toward the back door. Thirty-four's body left some smears of urine along the floor in spots. Rahim decided that whoever cleaned up would take care of it. He just wanted to get out of there as quickly as he possibly could and be done with the whole thing. They hadn't even left and already he wanted to get away from it all. To forget what he'd done.

Before they reached the door, Thirty-four's body tensed and Rahim and Safa both let go of his legs, which fell to the floor making a slapping sound. Thirty-four opened its eyes and lifted its head to look at Rahim, sending a shock of fear and terror through his body. Rahim quickly backed away, but Thirty-four's head went slack and cracked against the floor. Rahim glanced at the clock on the wall but didn't recall when he had given Thirty-four the shot. It couldn't have been more than a few minutes, perhaps that movement was his last. "Let's get this over with."

Safa punched the keypad and shoved open the back door. He held the door as Rahim dragged the body out toward the open rear doors of the van. He could have picked the boy up, but the stink of its body and the dampness of its fur because of the piss wasn't appealing on any level. After dragging the body out the back, he let it lie on the pavement while Safa turned off the bank of lights and closed the door. Then the two of them lifted the body into the van and closed it up.

* * *

Maria took the binoculars from Ten's hand. "What the hell was that?"

"A Humanzee," Maria said as though Ten had forgotten.

"I know, but…"

Once the van pulled away, Ten and Maria, with their hoods still pulled up and onto their heads, rushed toward the back door. Maria stopped with her hand held over the PIN pad and turned around, waiting for Ten.

"Six, three, three, seven, two, five," Ten repeated.

After she finished with the security code, a green light went on, and Ten pushed the door open.

Chapter 11

With his flashlight in hand, Ten led the way into the lab. They both wore their hoods well over their faces to increase the shadow. Cameras hung on mounts at two different locations against the front wall as they walked in. He hit each with his laser pointer to obstruct the optics prior to lowering the hood of his sweatshirt. Maria closed the door gently before walking deeply into the lab behind Ten. She switched her flashlight on, then copied Ten's moves for the first ten feet. The EXIT light over the door created a soft red glow of light, reaching into the space before them. A few cages clanged with the movement of small animals they couldn't see. Ten heard a low moan and wondered what animal might make such a sound. The odor of excrement lingered just beyond the obvious smell of air fresheners, which were probably set on timers around what looked like part laboratory and part kennel. He shone his light ahead of him as he stepped carefully and quietly.

"Over there," Maria said. Her flashlight beam pointed toward four large twelve-by-twelve cages. One child-sized Humanzee sat inside each of three cages; the last one was empty. All three of the small creatures had their faces buried into their arms like children shying from the light. The scene struck Ten as odd. Why would they be caged if they're children? What danger could they be? He also wondered why none of them stood or stirred. He looked over at Maria and cocked his head in question.

She gave him her usual shrug.

"I think they're mourning," he said.

"For the one we saw carried out of here." Her voice remained low. "What could have possibly gone wrong?"

Ten let the light from his flashlight wash over each of the Humanzees one at a time. The beasts were hairy like chimps, but had the physiques of humans: straight backs, shorter arms, human-like feet. Patches of brown skin showed through almost as though the fur was falling out, although that didn't appear to be the case because it wasn't patchy. They each had the same bare areas along their shoulders and upper backs. He couldn't see their fronts. And they were naked, even though it was a bit chilly in the space they occupied. "Let's take a closer look," Ten said as he walked around a bench and almost slipped to the floor. He bent down to examine the moist spot, sniffed before putting his knee on the floor, and wrinkled his nose. "Piss."

"What's wrong?"

"Nothing's wrong. I meant that I smelled piss; that's what this wetness is. Nasty."

"You're lucky that's all it is. They have small toilets in the cages. No wonder it stinks in here." Maria walked past Ten, giving him a wide berth as she got closer to the Humanzees. "The cages have numbers," she said. "Twenty-eight, Twenty-nine, Thirty-one, and Thirty-four, which is empty." She waved the flashlight around. "They took number Thirty-four out." She turned from the cage door. "I wonder what happened to some of the other numbers missing. And I wonder if Thirty-four just died? Maybe they were just removing the body."

"No," one of the other Humanzees said in a strong yet childlike voice.

Ten jumped back and hit his hip on one of the benches, rattling the bottles on its top. "Holy shit. They talk." One bottle fell over. Luckily, it was capped. Ten reached out and set it upright again, his hand shaking slightly as he did so. "Sounds like they talk." His voice also wavered with nervousness, and his head spun with questions concerning why he and Maria were even there, what they would do next now that they'd found the Humanzees, and what the beasts standing before him meant on a larger scale about humans, apes, hybrids. "I don't know," he said out loud, answering only some of the questions rattling around in his brain.

Maria stood with her mouth gaped open, then turned to Ten. "I don't know either. I don't think I actually believed they would be real. And here they are. Now what?"

He had no idea what questions she struggled with—probably moral ones. Or worry for the girls who had to bear these beasts. Either way, he felt as dumbstruck as she looked at the moment.

After it sunk in that the things could communicate, Ten rushed toward the talking Humanzee. His head had lifted from his knees. Ten angled his flashlight beam so it wasn't in the thing's face. He held up his arm as if to protect his eyes. His arm was hairier at the top than near the forearm and wrist, then fur grew on the back of his hand, as well as on top of his feet and on his thighs and rump. His calves were less hairy. And his face…

Ten approached the cage warily. "You talked." He lowered the beam even more and Twenty-eight lowered its arm. He had a thick brow with bushy eyebrows and tightly cropped hair over most of his flattened skull and face, except for his protruding, chimpanzee-like mouth, which was bare, as were the high points of his cheeks and nose. He looked more like a Neanderthal—at least judging from pictures Ten had seen—than a chimpanzee or a human. Except that his eyes glowed with intelligence, which was disturbing to see with him in such an inhospitable place. The animal's gaze unsettled Ten. "Your friend?" Ten cocked his head. "Was he killed?"

The boy Humanzee rose from his sitting position with astonishing grace. He stood tall and upright, like any young man you might meet on the street. He took two steps closer to Ten, then stopped. Thirty-one let out a small gasp. Twenty-eight pointed toward the wall and said, "Stick first, then stab." He made a thrusting motion with his right hand crossing over his body and poking into his left shoulder with an outstretched index finger.

Maria, who stood behind and to the side of Ten, waved her light over the wall where Twenty-eight had pointed. "Taser," she said. "They tased Thirty-four, then must have given him a shot to kill him. They couldn't have stabbed him. There isn't any blood. And the way he has his finger out looks like a shot too."

"Makes sense," Ten said. "But why? Was he diseased?"

"Makes sense," Twenty-eight repeated.

Ten continued to train his flashlight near Twenty-eight. Something strange, disturbing, and yet familiar stood out about the boy Humanzee. "They must be training them to speak. I wonder how much they are aware of themselves and the world and how much is just repeating what they've heard. I mean, they look old enough to speak in sentences. And he definitely looks intelligent." He looked at Maria. "And he answered us."

"Where's your mother?" Maria asked.

Twenty-eight stared at her as though trying to process the question, his brow furrowed.

"They must have taken them from their mother right away," she said. "They all look to be about four or five years old, but they don't speak very well. I suspect that the crossbreeding has affected their intelligence, but can they be trained to obey orders? That might be why they're here. They're test versions."

"Or does their personality lean toward the wild." Ten already felt as though he wouldn't want to be in the same room with one of them if were out of the cage. "If those men killed that other one, something must have gone wrong."

"I wonder if they turn crazy past a certain age." Maria conjectured. "After all, they are wild animals. At least part of them."

"No." Twenty-eight shook its head with a quick motion, then stared at Maria again. "You teach?"

Maria shook her head but didn't answer.

"Their teachers must be women." There was no knowing how smart they truly were. How much they understood their conversation, so Ten asked the question. "Do you understand us?"

Twenty-eight didn't answer, just stared at him, which didn't help him feel any more at ease. Finally, he couldn't look into his face any longer. He looked sad, confused. Ten turned to Maria. "We found out what we needed to know. We should go, let Jacob know our findings, and go to stage two if he still wants us involved."

"Ten?" Maria waved her light beam toward the cage.

Ten turned around and Twenty-eight stood wiping its eyes with the palms of its hands. It was crying. "Shit," Ten said, the action of the beast tearing at his heart. He walked closer to the cage. "Are you all right?" He hesitated with one arm raised, almost touching one of the bars, then backed up a few feet. He motioned for Maria to come closer. "It talks to you. It appears to be afraid of me."

"No wonder, if the men are in charge of…" She didn't finish the statement. She walked closer to the cage and placed a hand onto the bar. "What is it?"

Twenty-eight sniffled and turned away. "They killed him," he said very plainly. "Rahim killed him."

Chapter 12

Ten sat in Jacob's office, leaning forward in his chair with his elbows on the desk in front of him and his hands stretched toward his friend as though pleading with him. "You've got to help us get those things out of the animal clinic. Please. We have no idea what they're doing to them, what experiments they're performing. The conditions are terrible. If you can't help us, help them." He shrugged and brought his hands closer and gripped the edge of the desk. "What else do you want from us?"

Jacob looked calm, but his jaw clenched every few minutes, belying the tension between them.

Ten wanted to feel sorry for Jacob, but he couldn't. He was being stonewalled and didn't like it. For the past hour he'd been trying to push Jacob over the edge, knowing full well that it wasn't going to work. He hoped that either Jacob would break down and offer some kind of official help or tell Ten why he wasn't going to. The real reason, not some bullshit about the agency's inability to answer every call. But Ten was wearing thin too. He wasn't the type of person to hammer and hammer and hammer, although that's what he did.

"There is too much at stake," Jacob said before his jaw relaxed.

That meant nothing. It explained nothing.

Ten gave him the space he needed by sitting back in his chair, still straight, still with his head forward, but a little less threatening and confrontational. "I'm listening."

"There is a lot of tension between us and the Iranians. There has been for a long time, you know that. We can't accuse their government of such a heinous crime without tons of proof. We have to be positive. What if it's a privately run operation? We'd be in big trouble accusing the government."

"We have the clinic and the Humanzees themselves," Ten stressed.

"But we don't have informants. We don't have the head honcho."

"Dr. Shirazi? Dr. Clarkson?"

"The proof for Clarkson is sketchy—packages sent. And Afshan Shirazi is most likely caught in the middle somehow. Threatened. By the sounds of your first meeting with him, he's scared to death, or maybe of death. Maybe whoever is behind this is simply using his facility. I want important people. Those two might be able to tattle on the person we really want. If you can get them to do that, I *may* be able to step in." He looked away and took a deep breath before turning back to stare at Ten. This time Jacob leaned forward and whispered. "Even if we nab the person they're working for, it may not lead us to the top people, and it definitely won't lead us to the abductions of the surrogates." He nodded at his own words. "And that's what Maria's most interested in, isn't it?"

"I don't know how the hell you put up with this after being such an amazing engineer."

Jacob cracked a smile and turned to face a photo-realistic painting of an F-4 Phantom jet, Air Force issue. "I wonder too, sometimes. But I'm here, and right now I'm covering your ass. You shouldn't even be here, but that's too late." He talked to himself. "Probably a good thing. I'll have to tell people who you are."

Ten knew Jacob had given all he could. The ball was in Ten's court. The main reason he got involved in the case was because it was so important to Maria. He felt he owed her that much. He glanced away. He felt his face flush. Was his friend using his feelings of guilt to manipulate him? Although he and Jacob were friends, their friendship had only grown recently, and Ten still understood that Jacob could be a good liar if he chose to be. He stared at the man for a few moments and Jacob didn't budge. "I don't like this feeling," Ten said. "If anything goes wrong… a vigilante has no legal backup."

"I understand," Jacob said. "You can quit any time you want. I won't hold it against you."

Ten had hoped he'd offer more of a sense of commitment, but he didn't. "And every step closer we get to solving this the more dangerous it gets for both of us." Tapping the table, he said, "I don't care about me…"

Jacob blinked.

Ten knew this was difficult for Jacob as well. They had found the Humanzees caged in the laboratory of the Exotic Animal Clinic and there appeared to be nothing they could do to help the poor young beasts. Jacob might have been chief of staff at ISTI, he might have a lot on his plate but he wasn't heartless, and that's why Ten came to see him in the first place… seemingly to no avail.

"I'll step in if we get close enough to the source, or if you or Maria get in real danger. You know that, don't you?"

"How will you know if we're in danger?"

"I can't tell you that," Jacob said. Then a huge smile spread across his face.

Ten laughed out loud. "I don't fucking believe it, but I'm not finished with this yet. We'll get your contacts, your proof, your informants, or whatever you need to step in officially. You can count on it."

"You're not working for ISTI. Isn't that what you wanted?"

"Independent," Ten said. That was the word he remembered Jacob using, wasn't it? Or was it freelancing? Either way, it really meant that he was outside the law until he got paid, which would implicate them all. "I'll talk with Maria, let her know your stance. I felt I had to try. If not for my sake, then for hers. She deserves better."

"You can't make that decision, only she can. Besides, she's the best person to be working with you anyway; you know that don't you?"

"She understands the medical stuff," Ten said.

"Yes, but more than that, she's passionate about digging to the very end. She has a moral obligation and moral obligations don't allow one to just give up partway through. She'd be in on this whether we were or not."

"You're probably right." He nodded. "I know." Ten stood and stepped to the side of the chair. He reached to shake Jacob's hand. "I don't think you're handling this the right way, but it's your choice."

As they shook hands, Jacob said, "You don't have to agree with me. I'm okay with that."

They let go of each other.

"You'd better be there when we need you. For Maria's sake." Ten pointed his finger at Jacob's heart, then leaned in and poked him. "If something happens to her and I'm still alive…"

"I gave you my promise," Jacob said.

Ten left the office and walked down the hall toward the elevator. He pushed the down button, waited, and stepped inside when the doors opened. He stood there alone, and the weight of his decision fell across his shoulders and neck. The investigation *was* dangerous, and someone *could* get hurt. He scratched his shoulder. He didn't care what happened to him, but he did care what happened to Maria. She was innocent and so many bad things had already happened to her. He wondered, what Jacob was thinking? How could his friend put them in such a predicament? The pressures must have been enormous for him.

Ten scratched his shoulder again and noticed a dot of blood on his shirt where he'd been cutting himself. The healing itched and he must have broken a scab. After getting into his car, he drove to Mutual Consolidated Labs. The sun was high and warm. The air thick with humidity. It was almost noon. From the parking lot, he called Maria from his cell phone to ask her to lunch. "I talked with Jacob this morning about him taking over," he said over the phone.

"How did that go? I can only imagine." She sounded doubtful about the conversation he'd had with Jacob.

"We're getting in deeper than is safe," Ten said. "I don't know how I feel about continuing on."

"Yeah, that happened the night we broke into the Dr. Shirazi's animal clinic and found the Humanzees. Are you getting nervous?"

"Look, we can talk about all this through lunch. I can let you know what Jacob said and what I think, and we can talk about the dangers and our part in it. How does that sound?"

"Peachy. I won't be taking lunch until 12:30 today though. I have a project I want to get finished and I'm almost there. Does that work for you?"

"Yeah, I can wait in the parking lot. Back right corner under those trees."

"While you're waiting, it's a perfect time to call Dr. Olmstead."

"That again?" Ten said.

"Until you make the call. I'd make it for you, but you wouldn't go if I did that. Please. If we're going to be working together for a while, I want you to see someone." There was a short pause over the phone. "I worry about you," she said more quietly.

"No need to worry."

"Then call. Prove it to me."

Ten wanted to cry. He hated what he was doing to himself, but he also felt justified in doing it. He understood on an intellectual level that self-mutilation was a bad thing, but on an emotional level, he felt vindicated. Did he want some psychiatrist digging into his life when he was trying to forget it? He still wasn't sure, but he said yes. Why? Because he didn't want to disappoint Maria. And maybe that was the stronger feeling. Not that he cared for Maria in any romantic way, and he didn't get those feelings from her, but he felt she had been through enough already, partly because of him, and he didn't want her to go through any more heartache. "I'll call," he said.

"See you at 12:30." She hung up.

Ten was glad she didn't make a big thing about her getting her way. That would have made his decision feel wimpy, like he gave up. And he never gave up.

Chapter 13

Ten left a garbled, confused message for Dr. Olmstead, then got out of the car and took a walk around the parking lot. He wished he were home. Even though his last few months were spent feeling sorry for himself, learning where to mutilate his skin in a place difficult to see, and generally being a sloth, he just didn't know what to do with himself in the parking lot while waiting. He tried to focus on nature. The trees kept part of the lot shaded, which was chilly, and the sun kept other parts bright and a bit warmer. A soft breeze cooled his skin while in the sunny parts and made him shiver when walking in the shade. The air did smell good and the birds flitted about gaily as though he weren't even there.

Enough. It wasn't working. He only felt more anxious.

So he considered what he had gotten himself into, what little help Jacob and the ISTI organization were, and Maria's interest in the project. Her passion was what got her involved and he knew it. Jacob, even though he was chief of staff, appeared to have little control or he had control but not resources. Why else would he go outside, reach out to Ten? Finally, back to himself. What was he looking for? Why was he there at all? He claimed it was for Maria, but was it? He scratched his head and kept his eyes to the ground in front of him as he wandered around the parking lot a third time. Maybe he just needed to feel useful. He touched his shirt pocket and felt Dr. Olmstead's business card under his fingers. He could always discuss that with her. He had to laugh at himself after that thought. Already he was looking forward to the meeting. Maria had snuck that through.

By 12:30, he was back in the car and waiting, not as patiently as he'd like. He fiddled with the windows, then looked things up on his cell phone, like where they might go to lunch. There was a small food court down the street where he thought they'd find something they would both enjoy for lunch. It was close, even though at 12:30, he thought it might be busy.

When he saw her leaving the building, he started the car and drove to meet her. "You look nice," he said as she slid into the passenger seat.

"Work clothes," she said.

"I don't usually see you like this. It's nice."

"Well, I'm glad you like it." She shifted a little sideways in her seat and stared at him as he drove out of the lot. "So are you going to tell me?"

"Did you finish your project?"

"Small talk first, I see."

"Okay, okay. He held his ground."

"What's that mean?"

"He needs us to dig deeper into the arrangement, find the leader, or get one of the doctors involved to snitch on everyone. He said he can't help until there's more information about the project. Just finding the Humanzees isn't enough, I guess. And he doesn't want us going to the police or exposing any of this yet. It sucks. Besides, without at least one person with some authority or inside information, we'll never get lead to the girls they're bringing in as surrogates." He waited in case she wanted to say something, but she just sat there staring at him, probably waiting for him to finish. "And that's what's most important to you, right?"

"It's all important," she said. "Whether they're kidnapping girls and impregnating them with these beasts or they're creating an army of Humanzees aimed at killing our soldiers. Both sides are horrific. Both sides take the mind of a madman if you ask me." She turned toward him with a serious look. "How can we do this to each other? To other human beings? Not us specifically, but humans to humans?"

"I don't know," Ten said. "How can our own government be involved with technology that can literally kill millions of people? And I don't just mean the new technologies that ISTI is monitoring, I mean nuclear missiles we already have stockpiled. Why are humans so bent on destruction? From the start…"

Maria smiled at him. "We could go on, but we'd only be bitching and not helping."

"I guess we could. We've both been through plenty." He pulled up in front of a sandwich shop and parked his car. Looking up and down the row of buildings, he asked, "Where do you want to eat?"

"This is fine. I'll get soup or a salad."

"There's a whole row of places. You don't have to settle. I just parked in the first spot I saw."

"It's lunch, Ten, I think I can find something anywhere we go."

The line wasn't as long as Ten thought it might be. They ordered separately. Maria waved and said hello to a few people while they got their food and sat together near the front window.

"Work friends," Ten said.

"Associates," she said. "I don't call them friends."

He got the impression she didn't like her work but didn't want to ask the question outright. Before her statement, he had thought she liked working there. He picked up his BLT and took a bite. Then he popped a few chips into his mouth. He stared out the window as though he sat alone.

Maria dipped some bread into her soup and ate it.

The phone rang and Ten answered it. He raised his eyebrows toward Maria. Dr. Olmstead was on the phone making the arrangements. "Friday at ten works for me. Yes, it was Maria who recommended you. Thank you." He ended the call. "So you told her about me?"

"I hoped you'd call."

"By name, no less."

Maria shrugged. "Why wouldn't I use your name? Everything she does is discreet. I use everyone's name when I talk with her. She knows half of my workmates, Jacob and his group…" She took another bite of soup-soaked bread.

"I can only imagine what these psychiatrists know about everyone in town," Ten said.

"And they can't say a word," she said. "It would drive me nuts."

Ten ate more of his sandwich before saying, "Well, it's done. I made the appointment."

"You're saying that for your benefit, right? So you remember?"

"So you know and don't forget," he said. "When I need a favor…" He raised his water cup toward her in salute.

"Oh no, it doesn't work that way." She started to laugh. "I can't believe you'd hold this over me. I was trying to help."

Ten laughed with her. It felt good. He'd forgotten how to laugh. At least, he'd told himself that. "See, maybe you don't know me so well."

She reached out and put her hand on his forearm and they both stopped laughing. "I'm sorry," she said, removing her hand.

"No, it's okay, really. We're friends. It's just been such a long time."

She looked around the restaurant before returning his gaze. "I'm still having trouble blending in. I haven't laughed like that with someone for a long while either. I didn't mean anything by touching you. I hope you know that." She pointed to where she'd put her hand.

"I know. Do you miss Ben?"

"All the time." She gave him a quick smile then. "Just like you miss Amy."

He took a breath, realizing his breathing had become shallow.

"Anyway, I didn't mean anything. It's just that I felt comfortable for the first time in a very long time. And I'm so glad you called her. I want you to feel comfortable being alive too." She got serious again and stared at someone in line at the counter.

Ten turned to see who it was. "Who's that?" he asked.

"Dr. Clarkson's wife," she said.

"The receiver of the packages," Ten said. "I wonder how much she knows about what he's doing. Maybe she can be our informant. That might get the case over quickly."

"I don't think she knows much. I've talked with her a few times. Either she knows nothing, is a very good liar, or she's stupid as hell."

The woman, tall with brown hair and brown eyes, walked over with a to-go bag in her hand. "Maria, how are you doing?"

"Fine." Maria pointed toward Ten. "A friend of mine. Ten, this is Karla Clarkson."

Ten set down his sandwich and reached toward her. They shook hands briefly. She had a confident grip.

"Ten?"

"Stands for Tempest Eugene Nesbit," Ten said.

"Tem, then? Tempest," she suggested.

Ten smiled at her. If he had a nickel for every time someone got it confused. "My initials: T. E. N. My friends call me Ten."

"How clever," she said. "Well, it was nice to meet you. And nice to see you," she said to Maria before leaving.

"Odd," Ten said. "She didn't choose to talk with anyone else in here and there are others from your work."

"She knows something," Maria said.

"I don't like that. It puts you in danger." Ten sat back in his seat.

"Whoever is behind this must know that we broke into the clinic," she said.

"They might not know. They have no reason to review the videos of last night. After all, we used the keypad."

"You think the Humanzees would tell them?"

Ten felt instant concern. "If they're anything like human kids, probably."

"And now they know who we are," she said.

"But why would she pinpoint you? I took care of the cameras. How would she know?"

"Don't be an idiot. We went to see Dr. Shirazi together. He must have asked Clarkson about me, then he mentioned it to Karla, and there you go." She shrugged. "Doesn't matter. I don't care why. It just means that we've got to speed things up."

"Shirazi blabbed. Does that mean he's involved or scared?"

"Could be either, don't you think?" she said. "Maybe he just talked with Clarkson, asked about MCL, and Clarkson mentioned it to his wife. Any scenario is a bad one at this time. We don't need anyone being suspicious."

"I don't like this," he said. "You might want to stand back for a while. He's seen me, and now so has Karla. I'm sure it'll all get back to Shirazi too, and his boss. Even if they're only suspicious, we're in the line of fire."

CHAPTER 14

At lunch, Maria and Ten decided that Ten would go to see Dr. Clarkson to get a feel for what type of man he was and how cooperative he might be. Maria didn't need to be there for an initial assessment. His secondary goal involved finding out what Karla's piece in the puzzle was and if she was dangerous to anyone. Maria, particularly curious about Karla's involvement with the surrogates, told Ten that she felt eager to take the next step in approaching Karla. Was Karla the woman used to keep the girls calm while her husband went from one to the other? Was Karla to select which girls were the best candidates? Was her job more involved than to pass packages through MCL? Was she a real part of the operation or merely a go-between with no information? Had passing packages through MCL become transparent even to her? They considered their parts a one-two punch, reaching both of the Clarksons in the same day.

"Be careful," Ten said when he dropped Maria off at the lab.

"Be ready," Maria said. "Friday is two days away." Standing outside the car, she leaned over to look through the passenger side's open window. "You won't cancel, will you?"

"I'm worried about the Clarksons and you're more concerned that I'll cancel my head-shrinking appointment. Well, no, I won't cancel. I'm committed for now." He leaned over and reached to place a hand over one of hers, a recurrence of earlier at lunch. "Did you even hear what I said?"

"I'll be careful, but Karla doesn't appear to be dangerous."

"Not yet. You haven't cornered her."

"I'll give you that," she said.

He drove away after watching her enter the main building. It was a beautiful day, sunny and warming nicely. He drove straight home. Inside, he opened his laptop and called up some of his research on Dr. Clarkson, who appeared to be carrying on the experiments started by Ilya Ivanovich in the early 1900s. Dr. Clarkson had written several papers on Ivanovich's work. He'd also experimented with cloning. The man was very busy. He posted hours at his office as a general practitioner two days a week. His office was located in Dr. Clarkson's childhood neighborhood. It wasn't the best area, but it was where he grew up. Ten felt a liking to any doctor who would give back like that, which made him wonder why Clarkson would get involved in such a strange and creepy science like creating hybrid humans.

He printed some pieces out and wandered around his apartment for an hour or so, reading wherever he stood or sat. After a quick, mid-afternoon snack of a handful of potato chips, he decided it was time to go see Dr. Clarkson at his private practice. He had putzed around enough and wondered why something seemed to be holding him back, slowing him down. An internal feeling. He got a drink of water and ate an apple for his second mid-afternoon snack before making sure everything was closed up tight and walking out the door. He even fumbled with his keys when he locked the bolt lock.

He knew the neighborhood well enough to get into it and out of it fairly easily. Since his Taekwondo instructor taught in a small space at the opposite end of the strip mall where Clarkson held office hours, he stopped in to say hello, but the instructor wasn't around, and the doors were locked.

A sign said he'd be back, but Ten decided to park closer to Clarkson's office and avoid contact. The parking lot was sparsely populated, probably because two of the other stores in the strip were closed and had LEASE THIS SPACE signs in the windows. Yeah, he thought, someone's going to want to do that. Three cars were parked together at the far end of the lot and five guys stood around smoking and laughing.

Two patients sat in the waiting room when Ten walked in: a thin man with a pencil mustache who looked as though his cancer treatments weren't going well and a heavyset woman who looked as though her diet wasn't going well. A young woman sat behind the counter and off to the side, typing into the computer from what looked like notes from a patient file. "May I help you?" she asked without glancing up.

Ten leaned an elbow on the counter to look around at her. "I would like to talk with Dr. Clarkson. It's a matter of great importance to him."

"To him or to you?" the girl asked. Now she looked over, her face stern, her eyes offering no emotion.

"Both, most likely," Ten said.

"Are you a patient?"

"No, not really."

"I don't think he has any 'not really' patients. They either are or aren't."

"Then I'm not," Ten said, trying to be as soulless as she was being.

"Then what do you need to see the doctor about?"

A nurse entered the reception area and took a few folders from a flat file holder near the receptionist. She shuffled through them, found one, pulled it, and smiled up at Ten as she put the rest back. "And who might you be?"

He noticed her name was Georgia. He also noticed that she appeared overly interested in who he was. Unsure why that might be, he immediately took advantage of the eye contact and reached over the counter to shake her hand.

"The name is Tempest, but my friends call me Ten." He tried to enunciate the N the best he could.

"It's nice to meet you, Ten," she said. She had caught the pronunciation perfectly, which pleased him.

"I'd like to have a few minutes with Dr. Clarkson if I can," he told her in his most polite voice.

"I may be able to fit you between patients." She motioned him toward a door to his left. She walked around the receptionist, who rolled her eyes before Ten walked to the open door. Georgia held it open with her back and allowed Ten to walk past, almost brushing against her. "Right this way." She looked over her shoulder at him. "I would usually ask you to step into the bathroom and produce a urine sample, but I think we can skip that this time."

"I appreciate that," Ten said.

She opened an exam room door and said, "You can wait here for a few minutes. He'll be right with you."

Ten walked in and sat down on a short, round stool next to a counter with a sink located in the middle. He wasn't even sure what he was going to ask, or if he was going to ask anything at all. He mainly wanted to get a feel for what kind of man he was. It shouldn't take long. Yet he was well aware of how lucky he was that Nurse Georgia came along.

When Dr. Clarkson stepped into the exam room, he set a tablet and pen next to an empty folder he carried in with him. "Ten, is it?"

"Yes, sir."

He held up the folder with only Ten's name printed on it, and no last name or anything. "Well, we have nothing on you and I'm not taking new patients, but Nurse Ralston appears to think you need to talk with me about something. So, how can I help you?" He tilted his chin upward and took a breath. He was literally looking down his nose at Ten. He stood a normal height and sported dark hair, which was graying around the temples. He had hazel eyes and a soft demeanor—so far.

"You've been sending packages through Mutual Consolidated Labs and on to an animal clinic."

He hesitated only briefly before saying, "Oh, that. I produce artificial insemination services to the Exotic Animal Clinic. My friend over there, Afshan Shirazi, is an excellent doctor. My wife works at MCL and sterilizes some of the equipment I send over. She also checks for additional bacteria that may have been picked up from my clinic in the back here. I don't have the facilities necessary to package everything the way it needs to be, so I send it to her first."

"From here?"

"Exactly. I have a very small lab in a back room. She has a huge laboratory at Mutual Consolidated." He stopped and raised his eyebrows. "Is that all you needed? Are you doing some kind of investigation or something? If so, I can assure you I'm doing nothing wrong. I pay MCL for their work. Everything's legitimate."

"No, no. Well, yes and no. It doesn't really matter. You answered my questions."

"Well, then, I have to get back to my patients. You can find your way to the front desk." When he left the room, he heard Dr. Clarkson say, "There will be no charge," to someone, probably Nurse Ralston. He got up and wandered into the hall.

The nurse headed straight for him. "I'll walk you out," she said. When she got beside him, she whispered, "You might want to come back around 6:30." She smiled when he looked over at her. "After the receptionist leaves and there is time for us to talk privately."

Ten smiled. "I look forward to it."

She winked at him. "So do I."

CHAPTER 15

Abdi Karimi paced the floor in front of his desk, wringing his hands and breathing heavily. He could hardly believe the news he received. After so many years, what could have happened to expose them? Something was up. Someone—or some group—was onto the project, and possibly onto him. Now what? That was the question he asked his partner in crime, Mon, who hardly voiced an opinion until now. "Stop," he said. "Lay low for a while."

"How can I do that?" Abdi asked. "It's impossible. What do we do with everyone at the farm? Years of work, nurturing, developing. I am so close, so close to a huge sale. And the money is running out. I need to keep going."

"That is a dangerous proposition. What if our government finds out who is really involved? That you're research and production is here and not—"

"I know where it's not." He turned to the only other person in the room, Donya, the Humanzee trainer. "You're sure someone broke in while the cameras were down? You couldn't be mistaken?"

"No one can be positive. The men left a mess, a lot to clean up. But besides that, things didn't look right when I arrived. There was a skid mark…" She lowered her head.

"In the urine," Abdi said. "You told me."

"Rahim and Safa said they hadn't slipped. A few bottles were out of place too. It just felt wrong."

"But they dragged the body rather than carry it. Could that be it? Could they have knocked against a table and not noticed it?"

She shook her head. "Someone else was there. Twenty-Eight said something about people with lights. I showed him a flashlight and he confirmed it. Rahib and Safa didn't use flashlights; they turned on a bank of overheads. One of the intruders was a woman. I could tell the way Twenty-Eight ran his fingers through his fur when he told me about them. He was curious."

Abdi smiled at her. "You know these things quite well, don't you?"

A tear came to her eye. She didn't answer him.

Abdi turned around and yelled at Mon. "What the hell's wrong with her? She gets everything she wants from us, and now this, this sentimentality."

Donya spoke up. "You didn't have to kill him. I just wanted you to know the progress, the result of not feeding them. We could have worked with him. Don't you want to know how reliable they can be, how well trained? What if they're dangerous to the people who are fighting with them?"

Abdi glared at Mon while he talked to Donya. "I thought you'd be glad I got rid of him. He grabbed you."

"He wanted attention," she said.

Abdi said to Mon, "Your niece gets attached too quickly."

"She is a scientist. She's not attached, she's curious. And the death interrupted her experiments."

"Scientists don't cry over a failed experiment, they start a new one." Abdi cocked his head. "What about the two people who came to see Afshan?" Abdi pointed to Mon. "You know what we need to do about them."

"One of them works with Dr. Clarkson's wife at MCL. The woman, perhaps the one who visited, if Donya is correct that one of them was a woman. Karla and this other woman have been seen talking to one another," Mon said. "There is only one problem that I see. We promised Dr. Clarkson we'd leave his wife out of it. It was part of the agreement—"

"Which is over," Abdi interrupted. "We knew what Clarkson wanted. Has he gotten it? Is she pregnant? Check on that. If she's pregnant, then our agreement is complete. It's been years. He's had multiple chances. We've spent millions on his equipment. Clarkson's had all the time he needed, all the money we could spare. Things are tightening down now. We have to move quickly and get out. We have another order of surrogates coming through. We have the nursemaids weaning last year's Humanzees. And we have the younger ones. They're starting to live longer. Get them all on planes and out of here. Do it through Shirazi. Ship them all back to Iran. We can finish our experiments through interbreeding. We don't need these doctors any longer. How old is our oldest?"

"Five," Donya answered. "But you can't interbreed them."

"The hell we can't," Abdi said. "We'll wait until puberty." He felt unsure if he could hold enough of them that long.

Then Donya explained, "They're all sterile."

Abdi's hands went up violently over his head and came crashing onto his head in disbelief. "Why didn't I know that?" Abdi rubbed his face with his hands. He stepped closer to Donya and stared into her face, close enough to feel her breath. "We've been at this too long already to keep that secret."

He turned to Mon in frustration. "Tell her she can go."

Mon obliged.

After she left the room, Abdi sat heavily into the seat behind his desk. "You have been my friend a long time, Mon. Your council has been wise, but I must insist that we fulfill our mission." He tried to sound calm but felt the strain in his voice. The new information worked its way deeper into his mind. "We show our buyers the ones we have, sell them and all the pregnant girls, and disappear. Quickly. We won't get as much, but we have proof that the experiments work. We have the oldest ones who are still alive." He tapped the desk in front of him. A pistol always sat somewhere on the desk. Blood had been spilled many times in that room from that gun. He spun the gun with his index finger, and it made a couple rounds. "Send someone to stop this woman from MCL and her friend, whoever he is. Find them and stop them. We have them on video from the first time they visited Afshan, do we not? If they were smart enough to knock out our cameras at night…"

"We can't be sure that the same people came during the day and at night." Mon nodded. "I disagree with this plan of yours."

"They know about us. We must send a message."

"That might anger whoever is behind this."

"But it will also slow them down," Abdi said. "Kill them."

"I will carry out your orders," Mon said.

"I know you will."

"What about the two doctors?"

"We complete the last inseminations. One last shipment." He picked up the pistol and pointed it at Mon. "Then we don't need them. We disappear."

"They've never seen us," Mon said. "We don't have to kill them. And if Clarkson's wife is pregnant, I don't feel comfortable killing her husband after giving our word."

"You are getting soft like your niece."

Mon shook his head in disagreement, even while Abdi pointed the pistol at him. He showed no fear. "I was merely thinking of my own wife and children. Perhaps you might think of yours. How would that change your decision?"

"Perhaps I'll postpone that decision," Abdi said. "We'll see. First, we get rid of these investigators, whoever they are."

Mon didn't respond.

CHAPTER 16

Ten parked near his Taekwondo gym and waited until he saw the receptionist leave the doctor's office. He checked his watch: 6:30, almost on the nose. He remembered her face and hair, plain; her demeanor, solemn. She walked as though she'd been sitting all day, awkward and off-balance. Although she had appeared to be rather average in height and weight while behind the counter, in the open and while walking to her car Ten noticed she appeared heavier from the waist down than from the waist up. He wondered, briefly, what it was about the human anatomy that made some people carry their weight in one place and another person carry their weight in a completely different place? Not that it mattered, but it crossed his mind. He tended to hold weight around his torso, which made him feel thick if he binged for several days.

He laughed at his own wonderings as the receptionist climbed into her car and drove out of the parking lot. Once her car was out of view, Ten moved his car closer, locked it, and casually approached the office. The door swung open even before he arrived at the sidewalk.

"Hurry up. I need to lock the door," Georgia said as she held the door wide with one arm.

Ten rushed up and over the sidewalk and through the open door. Georgia closed and locked it in one smooth motion. "Let's go into the back to talk." She rushed past him and toward the door next to the receptionist's counter. At the last minute, she turned. "You coming?"

Suddenly, Ten wasn't sure what he'd gotten himself into. Nurse Ralston didn't appear as upbeat and happy as she had during the day. "Where we going?"

"To Dr. Clarkson's lab. I have something to show you. Isn't that what you wanted?"

He nodded quickly and headed for her. He had left his Glock in the car and suddenly felt naked without it. Not that he would need it if Nurse Ralston got aggressive with him, but he had no idea who else might be in the building waiting for him. What if she were in on whatever this was? What if he had just walked into a trap?

She burst through the door, walked briskly down past the patient rooms, and through another door. As it opened, Ten saw lab benches inside. All types of equipment sat around the room, on the floor and on the benches. As he entered, the space appeared to get smaller rather than larger due to all the bioelectronics equipment stuffed into the room. "This is a very small lab for some of the work Clarkson has been doing."

"You don't need a lot of room when working with… you know. Plus, part of the reason he sends stuff through MCL is to get it out of his way, I think. He can't keep everything here."

"And…?" He sensed she had more to say and waited.

Georgia smiled. "I like you, Ten. But what's your shtick? I could tell right away that you were concerned about something more than what you tell people. Not that you tell anyone any more than they need to know." She cocked her head. "You're looking for something. What is it?"

"I asked first," he said. "What's the other reason Clarkson sends stuff through MCL?"

Georgia walked closer to Ten and reached for his shirt collar. She stroked it as though it were a friendly cat. "You have to promise me that you'll spill your beans after I spill mine." He could smell her breath, sweet. "Promise?"

Ten felt uncomfortable with her so close, but he also felt a little flattered. Her interest in him as a man came through with her every move. But why him? "I promise," he answered. He thought he'd take things one step at a time until she showed her cards.

She smiled, let go of his collar, and walked over to one of the benches. She opened a drawer and removed a three-ring binder. She placed it on the bench. The photo of a child smiling broadly had been slid under the plastic on the cover.

"Who's that?"

"Dr. Clarkson's son." She stepped back for him to get a better look.

"I didn't know he had a son. My research didn't bring that up."

"If you looked online, that's why. He's so prolific within the scientific community that it's difficult to find personal information. It continues to fall lower and lower in the search engine. Part of that might be on purpose."

"I checked Wikipedia," he said.

"Oh, well, that's easy, isn't it? He protested and removed most of his personal data from there. That was easy. He included enough personal information about his parents and siblings, research and awards, that the write-up sounds honest, but it isn't.

"So, how about Karla? Did you find much about her? Probably not."

It was logical now that she mentioned it, and Ten felt stupid for not checking on her too. "I didn't look," he said a little sheepishly. To get back on topic, he said, "So, what about their son? How old is he?"

She reached over and, while saying the words, opened the binder. "Let's see."

Ten didn't like the sounds of those words. As she paged through, there were mostly photos of Clarkson and his son, sometimes his wife and son, and sometimes all three. The pictures had been taken everywhere he'd expect: at playgrounds, in the living room of their home with a Christmas tree in the background, entering school for the first time. Eventually, though, a number of pages in, there were photos of the boy in the hospital. Not too far after that, the boy lay flat in bed, one arm extended weakly, giving the camera the thumbs up. Ten didn't need her to go much further to know that the boy died. He placed a hand over the page to stop her. He looked at Georgia. "I don't need to see any more."

She moved his hand aside. "Yes, you do."

Ten tentatively watched as she turned a few more pages. The photos were gone, now between the plastic sleeves lay pieces of paper with formulas and charts. Some were labeled, but not all of them. One was labeled KARLA. "What's all this?"

"You know what he does for the Exotic Animal Clinic?"

"More than you might realize," Ten said.

Georgia raised her eyebrows and smiled. "I'm looking forward to your disclosure even more now." She closed the notebook and placed it back into the drawer, then leaned against the bench to square up with Ten. "In this lab, he performs several studies, some with animal sperm and some with human cells."

"His work with clones…"

"Yes, and his work with artificial insemination." She sounded clinical all of a sudden.

"He's trying to clone his son, then inseminate Karla so that she can birth him all over again." Ten felt shock rush through him as he said the words aloud. It reminded him of how people in the seventeenth and eighteenth centuries would name their secondborn the same as their firstborn if their firstborn died before the second was born. That happened with Van Gough, and Ten always wondered if that wasn't a huge burden on the secondborn. It all seemed so barbaric to him now. And this cloning thing felt worse when he thought about it.

He was still digesting the whole concept when Georgia said, "Your turn."

He couldn't let go of the thought that easily. "Why would they do that?"

"They want the same boy, not another one. And it's illegal to clone a human, you know that." She was close to him again. "Okay, you got in a bonus question. Now it's your turn."

He took a breath. "I'm an independent contractor. My job, at this moment, is to research and learn more about… well, about what you've just shown me. It goes much deeper than that though. Clarkson appears to be involved—is involved—in creating crossbreeds between men and monkeys. Chimpanzees, to be precise. He's helping someone create an army we believe. An army of Humanzees."

Georgia laughed out loud. "You've got to be shitting me?"

Ten looked directly at her. Her reaction confused him. Wouldn't she understand what he said better than anyone? "Not at all. I've seen them."

She turned away. "You've seen them?"

"Yes, my partner and I visited the Exotic Animal Clinic. They're about six years old or so; we're not sure. They look a lot like chimpanzees, but they stand upright and they talk."

"They talk?"

He nodded and stopped talking. He may have said too much. What might she do with the information? "You are sworn to secrecy," he said out of desperation.

Georgia laughed again. "Yeah, like anyone would believe this. And I thought cloning his own son was weird." She shook her head in disbelief. "That's where he gets the money, then."

"The money?"

"What he's doing sounds awful," she said.

"That's not the worst of it. Whoever he's working with is abducting young women, often girls, to be the surrogates."

"Oh my God." Georgia put a hand over her mouth. She was no longer laughing. "Who would…?"

"That's what we're trying to find out."

She walked away from him and stopped. "It all makes sense now."

"What does?"

"The doctor has had quite a few visits lately. One just today. Two or three foreign men stopped by to talk with him. He always looks distraught afterward, but I never ask questions. I've learned, after his son's death, not to disturb him about what he's doing. He's a very private man. I think that's why he keeps me around. I don't ask and he doesn't have to feel like he's hiding anything." She paused. "But he is."

"Why do you think those men showed up today?"

"I don't know. Usually he's expecting them, but not today."

"Was that before I showed up, or after?"

"After." Her eyes widened. "Do you think they followed you here just now?"

"No." He was sure of it. "But they are suspicious. Did you create a file on me? I saw one."

She smiled at him. "It has nothing but your first name on it. Ten. It's empty. I knew something was up, even before those other men visited after you left."

Ten thought for a moment. "Afshan Shirazi," he said. "You know that name?"

"Of course. We talked about the Exotic Animal Clinic. Dr. Shirazi is a friend of Dr. Clarkson's. They've worked together for six or seven years." Her eyes widened again, this time with recognition.

"Exactly," Ten said. "We visited him too." Ten turned around and looked along the ceiling rim. "No cameras in here?"

"Only in the front office," she said.

"Where's the video stored?"

"You look upset."

"Where's it stored?" he pressured.

She shrugged. "Offsite somewhere, I think. It's a service."

"Maria…"

"Who's that?"

"My friend on this case. She and I visited Dr. Shirazi. They have us on video. I have to go." He turned and headed for the door.

Georgia stepped up right behind him. "Do you think she's in danger?"

"Absolutely."

"Before you leave…"

"Yes?" He swung around and she stood right there, so close they could have kissed.

"Are you dating anyone?"

"Really?" he asked.

"I'm not usually like this, but I sensed something about you right away." She shrugged again and turned her eyes away as though totally embarrassed. The shyness of her motion was endearing.

"I'm not," he said. "Let me call you sometime. During work hours. But for now, you might not want too many people to know that you know me." He pointed toward a camera in the parking lot. "You let Clarkson know that I requested a private conversation about his work, that's why you let me in. That I seemed more interested in Shirazi." He touched her forearm lightly. "Stay safe."

CHAPTER 17

Ten called Maria as he walked through the parking lot toward his car. He held the phone tightly to his ear as he headed out of the parking lot. After five rings, it went into her voicemail. He tried again. She still didn't answer. While driving, he unzipped his backpack and wiggled his Glock 19 out of the main compartment and placed it on the passenger seat. He reached back in and fished around the bottom of the pack until he found both magazines he'd thrown in there earlier. He placed them on the seat next to the gun.

His conversation with Georgia rolled around in his head like so many pinballs. What was he to make of the information? It all sounded so insane. He could understand a man wanting his son back—it struck home for him—but why would a woman want to give birth to the same child a second time? It was creepy to the point of horrific. Didn't she wonder if the kid would die a second time? Didn't either of them wonder about that?

Ten hadn't even asked Georgia how Clarkson's son died. He assumed it was a disease, but maybe it was an accident. They could avoid an accident perhaps. Maybe that was their thinking, but a disease wasn't so easily sidestepped, not if they used the same genes for sure. He was no expert, but again, the whole situation was straight out of a horror novel.

His train of thought didn't take long to shift to his personal situation, to Amy carrying their unborn child. He hadn't even gotten to see his own daughter be born, and here

Clarkson was going to see his son born a second time. The situations overlapped too much for him. Even through the horrible idea, he could understand how any person might want to see their child one last time, or in his case, just once. To reproduce the child as Clarkson attempted though didn't seem plausible. Was it even possible? A close approximation wouldn't be the same as an exact duplicate. And an exact duplicate would be creepy. After all, the child won't have the same experiences. What if their child's personality was totally different? How would they handle that?

Ten thought deeply about the situation, about how much Karla must love her husband to do such a thing. Or was he doing it for her? It didn't matter. Love. It produced miracles and madmen. What other emotion could do such a thing? He knew that he would have done anything to save Amy. Anything. The men who came for him and his family even killed his dog. He watched the man shoot Groucho. He shook his head to try to eliminate the images, but it didn't help.

He burst into tears while driving toward Maria's house. He removed a hand from the steering wheel and balled it into a fist, then hit himself in the head and face several times. The pain he inflicted on himself still didn't ease the pain in his heart, which also exploded into his neck and head as tension and anxiety. He looked over at the Glock and shook his head at the thought that he knew crept behind his other thoughts. He would cut himself with a paring knife, he would punch himself in the face, but he wouldn't commit suicide and he knew it. Why? What was he living for?

Ten parked his car two blocks from Maria's house. He slapped a magazine into his Glock, stuffed the second magazine into his back pocket, and crammed the pistol in the back of his pants. He locked the car and ran through one of the yards, into a side yard, then through the backyards of several houses. He slowed as he approached Maria's house. There didn't appear to be anyone home from the back, so he crept close to the side and walked toward the front. Passing a window, he looked in and saw no one. He worried that he was too late, that they'd kidnapped her or killed her. How could he live with himself if that happened, if anything happened to her? Hadn't he caused enough trouble for everyone?

As he approached the corner of her house, Ten slid along the wall to peer around to the front. Her car sat in the driveway. Parked cars lined the street. Ten turned around and edged back to the side of the house, to the kitchen door. She lived in a safe neighborhood and often left that door unlocked, he remembered from when he used to visit her when he first arrived. He was right. Turning the knob slowly and quietly, he opened the door just enough to walk inside, then closed it just as slowly and quietly until it latched. He tiptoed across the kitchen toward the hall. From the living room he heard Maria say, "What do you want?"

"You need to come with us," someone said in a thick accent.

"Where? I don't want to go anywhere. You'll have to drag me and I'm sure the neighbors will notice."

"Don't do this. We are not going to harm you. We just want to talk," a second man said.

"Then talk," she said.

Ten heard her squeal and imagined her being grabbed by the arm.

"You're coming with us," the first man said.

If one person grabbed her, the two of them would be standing close together. He'd have to react quickly and accurately or she could get hurt, and he couldn't live with that. Most likely the person holding her would pull Maria in front of him the moment Ten entered. But how many people were with her? At least two. Shoot the other one, he thought. They couldn't both hide behind her. He got to his knees. They wouldn't expect him at that level, plus there would be a smaller area to aim at if they chose to shoot him.

She squealed again and he knew they were coming his way from the clarity of her voice. He had to hurry. On one knee, Ten scooted to the doorway, stuck his head around the corner, and the Glock a moment later. In an instant, he captured the image of the three bodies: Maria and two men. As expected, the man holding Maria pulled her toward him. Ten pulled the trigger and shot the other man in the chest. A loud thud and the man crumpled to the ground. He pulled back behind the wall, stood, and stepped away from the door jam.

The man holding Maria shot through the wall at about the level where Ten had been a moment before. Ten tried his best to make it sound as though he'd been hit, then moaned with his hand over his mouth. He waited to see if the man bought his act.

"Stay where you are!" the man yelled.

Ten moaned again.

"Push your gun where I can see it!" the man yelled.

Ten leaned over, set the gun on the floor and slid it into view. Then he stepped closer to the door jam, balled both fists, and waited. The man would push Maria through first. He would expect Ten to be on the ground, so he'd be looking down. Ten raised both fists above his head, ready to slam them into the man's skull. A moment later, Maria's body passed through the door. A large arm was wrapped around her shoulders and a gun was held out toward whatever the man thought he might find. Ten didn't even have to think about it; with the gun pointing away from Maria, he had a clear opening. He dropped his fists straight down and hit the man squarely on the crown of his head as hard as possible. He felt the man's neck collapse as the man passed out. The gun, in his weakened hand, folded over Maria's shoulder to the floor. She fell into Ten's arms. "Where do you learn this stuff?"

"I watch a lot of movies." He moved her away and said, "Let's tie this guy up and call Jacob to come get him."

She rushed back into the living room and grabbed her phone and pushed speed dial.

Ten checked to be sure the man was out solid.

As Maria walked toward him, she finished her brief conversation with Jacob and lowered the phone.

Ten looked up at Maria. "You can't be involved anymore."

"I am involved," she said.

"This just became too dangerous."

"It's too dangerous for you too." Her curly hair appeared to be moving, but then Ten realized she was shaking. He stood and held her for a few moments. "Are you going to be okay?"

"This is the part I never liked. Now I see why."

"Maybe a normal life isn't so bad," he suggested.

"I didn't say that." She let go of him. "I'll get something to tie him up with."

"Do you have wire ties?"

She stopped and looked at him. "Sure, in my electrical toolbox." She shook her head. "I'll find some rope or something in my junk drawer." She walked past him toward the kitchen.

Ten retrieved his gun and stuffed it into his pants again. He checked the pockets of the man who had passed out but didn't find anything. The man was clean. The other one was too. He collected the gun that had fallen on the floor and placed it near the doorway. There was only one weapon between the two of them. How strange. They didn't appear to be professionals, which didn't make sense if a foreign government was involved.

Maria came back with some clothesline rope. "Jacob should be here soon."

Ten reached out for the rope. "This'll have to do."

"What about him?" she asked, pointing to the other man.

"He's dead. I'm sorry. I had no choice."

"I'm sorry too. So who do you think they work for? They look Iranian. Not that I'd know that for sure, but that was our original guess, wasn't it?"

"Maybe Iranian; who knows at this point. I don't think there's a government involved in this anymore," Ten said while tying the man's hands.

"Who has the money to invest in such an elaborate scheme?"

"Don't know, but these guys aren't military. They aren't professionals at this. I don't get it. It's almost like they pulled a couple guys off some assembly line to come and get you." He shook his head at her as he made the last pull on the rope. "Who does that? Did the people involved in this actually think they'd get away with it? That they'd never get caught?" Ten rolled the man onto his side and pulled his feet back and began to tie them to the man's bound hands.

"Maybe they expected it to be short term. There is a lot of money in private hands, I'm sure."

"You may be right," Ten said. "They could have thought they'd move in, do some research—no one would ever question scientific research—then move out once they have enough Humanzees to start their own interbreeding."

"Except that they're probably sterile," she said.

"Why do you say that?"

"Crossbreeding typically creates sterile offspring. At least this type of crossbreeding, between species. Like mating a horse and a donkey. You get a mule. It's sterile. They've also inseminated a lion with a tiger to make a liger. Also sterile."

Ten pulled on the rope really hard. "That's not good."

"It's science," she said. "Maybe they don't know science very well and Clarkson has been cheating them. If so, he's in big trouble when they find out. I'm surprised they haven't found out yet."

"But that would mean they'd need surrogates, thousands of them, if they were going to create thousands of these beasts."

She stared at him, obviously while processing what he'd said. "They would have to use the same girls over and over again, year after year." She put a hand to her mouth. "How horrible. All this means is that we really have to stop them."

Chapter 18

Ten could tell that Maria was still a bit shaken, even when Jacob and two other agents showed up to help out. After some minor investigation and taking of clues, one of the agents went outside to find the car the men drove to Maria's to check the registration. Jacob walked into the kitchen where Ten and Maria waited. Ten looked up and asked, "You're through?"

Jacob turned and pointed toward the living room. "We'll have someone clean up completely in there. There were two calls that a shot was heard, and the police aren't happy with us walking in like this, but we've taken care of everything. You may have to move to a safer place for a few days," he said to Maria, "and you might have to as well," he said to Ten.

"Let them come after me," Ten said. Then he heard himself and lowered his eyes in embarrassment. He wasn't trying to be a badass. He just wanted Jacob to know that he'd be ready.

Jacob walked around the counter. "Yeah, well, we can't have that."

Ten met his gaze. "So you've got to report this to someone. And a few of your agents have seen me, questioned me. I guess that means all this is exposed now. Basically, we're off the hook." He glanced at Maria. "We can move on. Isn't that right?"

"Not quite," Jacob said.

Ten stared at his friend for a moment. "I don't get why that's not true. It's getting more dangerous. You said you'd take over at this point."

"I don't think this report will go in for a few weeks at least. Things get backed up when you're as busy as we are. You write reports when you can and that's not always right away. I can manipulate the rules when I have to, if that's what you're asking?"

Maria put her hand on Ten's arm. "It's okay. This was a minor situation. There are more important things to do still."

"You haven't stopped shaking since I arrived. You're through," he turned to Jacob, "even if I'm not."

"I've told you before. I'm going through with this… no matter what you want."

"I don't like it. Jacob?" He looked to his friend for help.

Jacob pursed his lips and then smacked them as though he'd just eaten something delicious. He ignored Ten's plea. "Will you continue to try to get through to the two doctors? All I need is one of them to squeal. We can catch the people behind this, the people behind the abductions, and close everything down before anyone actually knows something's going on."

"And Maria?"

Jacob took a deep breath and let it out slowly. He shook his head. "I can't make her do anything."

"You'd like to close this case, wouldn't you? But you need us," Ten said.

"My friend, I'd like to close every case I have, and probably a hundred I don't even know about yet. This situation isn't as bad as that killing machine we worked on together. It may not be as bad as several of the other cases we're working on at this very moment—in fact, it isn't that bad—but it's bad enough that I want it eliminated. And you two can do that, with very little of my help. Ten, I know you can do this with or without my help. I'd rather you do it without. I can't get involved right now."

"Not her," Ten said.

"Oh yes, her," Maria interrupted. "You can't use him to eliminate me from this. He already told you he can't control what I do, and neither can you."

"Look at her!" Ten said to Jacob, "She's still upset."

"I'll get over it. I'll be okay," she said.

Jacob stared back and forth at them. "I won't make that decision. You'll have to figure this out between you." He swung around as one of the other agents entered the room. His tone and demeanor changed to more casual. "In the meantime, we have to move you, both of you. I have a friend who will keep this quiet." He turned around and walked out of the kitchen. Ten heard him give orders to one of the other agents.

Maria came up beside Ten and pushed against his shoulder playfully. "At least this way I can keep an eye on you."

He wasn't amused. "You don't get it. This is serious now."

"I get it. But I refuse to let it stop me."

"Well, you won't be able to keep an eye on me like you think. Not permanently. There's a lot I can do without you, while you're safe."

"I'm so glad to hear you say that."

He smiled at her. "I'm sure you are."

Even before the agents' crew started cleaning up Maria's living room, the two of them were in a van headed toward the center of town. "Isn't it more dangerous if we're living together?" Ten asked the agent sitting next to him.

"We'll be guarding you twenty-four-seven."

"So you must be in on this. You must know our connection to Jacob."

"I only know what I'm supposed to know and none of that can I discuss with you," he said.

"And still reports aren't being made?" Ten asked.

"They're being made…"

Ten shook his head. "But no one has to see them unless they have the right security clearance, right?"

The man didn't respond.

When Ten didn't get anything more out of the agent, he reached out his hand. "You are?"

The man shook hands with Ten. "Agent Todd Daily."

Ten scrunched up his face. "I know that name."

"Nuclear physics," Todd said.

"What the…"

The agent straightened up and returned Ten's questioning look. "You do know who I work for."

"Yes, but it didn't used to be like this?"

"When they hired Jacob, he came in and changed the focus of ISTI completely. He's hired, let's say, a team more geared to the job. Driving is Agent Robert Martin. He has a PhD in mechanical engineering." Todd nodded. "I know about you." Then he looked at Maria. "And you."

"What about Jacob's boss, everyone above him? Are they equally as, should I say, selected?"

Agent Daily smiled, showing a lot of teeth. "The usual." He shrugged. "Can't get rid of all the bureaucracy."

"That's why Jacob keeps us out of the loop, so to speak," Ten said.

Agent Daily still didn't answer Ten directly. He just offered more information. "We like to think of it as a secret service within the secret service. Not that ISTI is secretive in all its operations, but there is a lot going on at our level that no one knows about. Not even those above Jacob. He understands how to manipulate funds and numbers. He's a brilliant man."

"We knew that," Ten said. After a long pause, he said, "But maybe I didn't realize it went so deep."

The van stopped. "We're here," Agent Daily said.

Ten opened the back of the van and stepped out into the bright light of the setting sun. Deep pink and orange blazed across the western sky over the top of a three-story apartment complex. He turned around and helped Maria step down from the van. Her eyes squinted at the bright light. Agent Daily exited last. The complex looked as much like a cheap hotel as an apartment complex. There were several different buildings, and each apartment came with a sliding door opening onto a small porch. Ten recognized the place and wondered how many of the renters were legit, now that he knew Jacob was friends with the owner.

Agent Daily handed Ten his backpack. "We'll take care of both your cars for now. In the meantime, you can continue your work as usual, but we can protect you better here where we're familiar."

"You mean while we're here you can protect us," Ten said. "When we're out, you can't."

"We'll be keeping an eye on you. But we won't interfere unless we feel it is absolutely necessary. You're running your own show, top to bottom."

"So you do know what we're up to," Ten said.

"I don't have to know anything to let you run your own show," Agent Daily explained.

"How reassuring." Ten and Maria followed Agent Daily into the building, up some stairs, and down a short hallway, instead of taking the elevator. "You're sharing this space for now."

"Oh fun," Maria said.

"Thanks, but no thanks," Ten said.

Maria leaned closer and whispered, "You're a flight risk and a self-mutilator, and you're worried about me? Really?"

"I get it. You don't have to be rude."

The apartment stood at the end of the hallway on the third, and top, floor. Agent Daily stepped into a small foyer, walked down a short hall, and stopped inside a living room with a vaulted ceiling and lots of windows. "Nice," Maria said. "I may want to move permanently."

"Isn't all this glass a problem?" Ten asked.

"Like I said, we'll be watching you."

Ten walked past the two of them and into the first bedroom. He opened a dresser that stood next to the wall and it had clothes in it. "Someone already living here? Or just moved out?" He grabbed a t-shirt and yanked it out. It was one of his. "Hey, what the hell? When did you guys know we were being moved?"

Agent Daily stood at the doorway with his hands on either side and his body leaning in. He glanced around. "We had both rooms equipped with some of your stuff, not everything, but you can ask for whatever you need. We'll retrieve it for you."

"I don't like people breaking into my apartment and grabbing my things."

Agent Daily shrugged but didn't answer. "Your room is the master," he said to Maria while opening the next room's door. "You have your own bath and…"

Ten stopped listening. He wasn't sure whether to be pissed or okay with the whole operation. Whether he should be concerned or glad. He walked into Maria's room a few moments later. "Couldn't you just monitor us in our own places?"

"Like I said, it's easier here."

"It's bugged then," Ten said. "We're being watched by our employer. Real nice."

"Settle down," Maria said. "It might be for the best right now."

He knew what she meant but didn't agree. He liked his freedom. Worrying about being watched all the time was going to put a damper on his activities.

CHAPTER 19

The next day Ten and Maria, who took a few days off work, drove to Dr. Clarkson's office. They argued halfway there because Ten was still adamant Maria shouldn't even be involved anymore.

"I'm not staying in that apartment alone any longer than I need to and you're as good a bodyguard as I suspect any of those physicists are."

"You may be right there," Ten agreed. "I'm still not happy with this arrangement though."

"You'll have to get used to it, to me, at least for now."

"Well, I am eager to know more about this whole cloning thing." Ten felt relieved that Maria was with him for that reason. She'd understand all the biomedical details they might obtain. And, being that she knew what she was doing, he thought Dr. Clarkson might talk more freely with her, maybe even get excited and spill more information than he wanted. Get into the artificial insemination practices he was into. The well-founded plan worked great in his mind. Then they drove up to the doctor's office and found it closed.

"Something's up," Maria said. "He has morning hours today."

"You think?" Ten parked and got out of the car where he felt like he could breathe more freely. Then he walked to the door.

"Where you going?" she yelled out the window.

"Checking…" He rattled the door and knocked, then cupped his hands to the window to see inside. No one was there. He glanced into the car at Maria, "I'm going to check in the back." Since the doctor's office was the right-side anchor to the strip mall, the building ended but the parking lot didn't. It wrapped around the building where a narrow alley was used for deliveries and pickups, as well as trash collection, which happened at the far end, near the Taekwondo gym. The odor was strong, even though the trash bins were a few stores down. He wondered how awful it must be to deliver packages to the rear of the building with such stench. Then he wondered how all that trash floating around might affect any medical tools or drug deliveries. Maybe that's why Dr. Clarkson sent things through MCL. Ten knocked on the back door and shook that handle a second time. He got the same answer. His first thought was to worry about Georgia and the receptionist. Were they okay? He jogged back to the car.

"How strange," Maria said sarcastically, "they locked both doors."

"Everyone who works there is in danger," Ten said. "And we have no help." He put a hand to his forehead and closed his eyes momentarily. "I don't like this arrangement at all."

"It'll be okay. We can alert Jacob and he can take care of them. I'm sure of it. I'm sorry." Maria turned her head away, then reached around to the backseat area and grabbed Ten's backpack from the floor. She unzipped it and removed the Glock. She set it on the console between them. "You may need this." She wasn't being sarcastic this time.

"I don't even know where to go."

"The Exotic Animal Clinic," Maria offered.

"I suspect—"

"But you won't know until we check." She pulled her cell phone from her purse. "I'll try calling ahead."

Ten drove from the parking lot toward the highway. The Exotic Animal Clinic was about an hour away. They'd have to pass Mutual Consolidated Labs, or near there anyway, on their way. "Check to see if Karla's at work too."

She stared over at him. "I hope so."

"So do I."

As he drove as fast as he was able through traffic, Maria found that Karla was indeed at work and glad to hear from Maria. She asked about the call, and Maria told her that she just wanted to be sure everyone got the message that she'd be out for a few days.

"Is everything all right?" Karla wanted to know. "You sound a bit distraught."

"Yes. I'm fine, thank you. I just need to be with my friend for a few days. He's going through a rough time."

"Well, you're a good friend. You take care of him, then."

They both hung up.

"She seems okay," Maria said.

"Why am *I* going through a rough time?" Ten asked.

"Because you are. And I'm here for you."

"Yeah, to make me keep my appointments."

"If that's what it takes."

"So, about Karla. Either she's a great liar, or whatever happened to her husband happened after they both left for work this morning," Ten said. "That means we have time to find him."

"Let's hope he's with Dr. Shirazi."

"That's your next call…"

She dialed and held the phone to her ear. She glanced over at Ten and he knew what that meant. No answer. He checked his watch. They had a half hour to go. "I don't like it."

"Should I call Jacob?"

"Yeah. I want him to check on the nurse and receptionist. But let's face it, he's not going to help us. I think he made that clear after you were attacked."

"He said they'd keep an eye on us. Are we being followed?" She turned around in her seat.

"Not that I can tell. Keeping an eye on us must be a euphemism for something else. Maybe he meant they'd check in on us once in a while or they'd watch us as long as we didn't go anywhere." He reached over and patted her thigh. "I don't like any of this. But I'll take care of you."

"I'm not worried."

"You were pretty shaken up yesterday."

"That was yesterday. Maybe I'm getting used to it."

"I'm not," Ten said. "I don't want to either…" He stared at the road ahead.

"That's what you're worried about. Aren't you?" she asked.

"Don't try to analyze me. It's much deeper than that."

"Then tell me."

He looked over and met her eyes. "No."

"Then tell Carol at least." He gave her a questioning look. "Carol Olmstead. The psychiatrist you're going to see at ten tomorrow?"

"Oh. We'll see how today goes first."

"You're not backing out now. You can't cancel at such short notice. Besides, you promised."

Ten pointed ahead. He didn't want to talk about any of it, or around it. If anything, he wanted to forget how he felt, what he was going through, and where it all might lead. But most of all, he didn't want to include Maria in his process any more than he had to. It would be bad enough to have to talk with the psychologist. He definitely didn't want to discuss his feelings while driving. What he really needed to do was focus on the task at hand.

In the parking lot, Ten got out of the car right away.

"Wait!" Maria yelled.

When Ten bent to look at her through the door, he saw her hand with the Glock 19 held out. He reached in and took it from her and stuffed it into the back of his pants and pulled his shirt over it.

Maria got out of the car and followed him.

"Why don't you stay back?" he suggested.

"Don't you think I'd be better protected if I'm with you? If anyone knows we're here or followed us, I'm a sitting duck in this lot. Plus, you have the gun."

"Fine. Let's go."

The clinic, unlike the doctor's office, was open. The two of them walked into the waiting room, the only ones without a caged animal or an animal on a leash. One woman had a ferret on a leash and it was eyeing a cat in a cage pretty suspiciously. Another person sat holding a terrarium with a yellow snake inside. Ten wondered how you might take a snake's temperature. And what was the normal temperature for a snake?

Maria asked for Dr. Shirazi and the woman at the counter asked if they had an appointment. Ten didn't recognize the receptionist.

Maria pulled her ID out and said, "We're from MCL. He called us. If I can't see him, I'm leaving, and he'll have to wait two weeks until I have another slot open. So, if he didn't tell you, that's not my problem."

The girl looked flustered. "Oh, well, let me check. He's in the back, and—"

"Why don't you just click your buzzer back there and we'll wait in his office as usual."

"Usual?"

"We've been here before," Maria said convincingly.

Ten was impressed the way she bullied through the opposition. The girl behind the counter appeared nervous and attentive. She did exactly as Maria asked and a moment later the two of them were walking down the hall toward Dr. Shirazi's office. But that wasn't who they met when they opened the door.

Chapter 20

Abdi had Maria's assailant, the one still alive, shot from a passing car so he wouldn't talk. Now the man who had done that job for him lay on the floor with a bullet in his skull. Abdi set the pistol on his desk, where it remained a threat.

Mon shifted in his chair. "You will exhaust your help if this continues."

"I don't need you telling me that you told me so." He spit on the floor. "I can buy more men, more women, as many as I need." He walked around his desk and toward Mon, but didn't confront him aggressively.

Mom raised his eyes to meet Abdi's gaze. He repositioned himself more comfortably. "You don't think the American government will come for you now? Your actions indicate that you're scared. That you're willing to kill your own people. I have told you before that your methods may not have the outcomes you would like."

"For my family. For our families!" Abdi held up a clenched fist. "We're almost there. We do this for more than ourselves and that is why my actions are justified. One more shipment of pregnant women. A total of one hundred Humanzees. That's all that was promised. By the time the resistance waits for these beasts to get to the proper age, our families will be safe, we will be old men—and untouchable."

Mon appeared to ignore Abdi's rantings. "We might want to move from here. Anyone who watches the clinic may follow one of the men to the farm and…" Mon let the sentence go.

Abdi didn't have to hear any more. He felt his anger grab his heart and squeeze. He owned the largest biochemical laboratory in Iran and could never do what Clarkson and Shirazi had done. And they refused to train Abdi's doctors. They kept their secret, kept their research between them. They knew that they held all the cards. Any threat, any harm to their families, would mean they wouldn't work together, wouldn't create the beasts that Abdi would sell to the resistance underground. He didn't have to know what they were going to do with the Humanzees. He could guess. His job was only to supply a product, just like any business.

He hated knowing the truth. That not one of his biologists had gotten anywhere near where Clarkson and Shirazi had gotten. And he wasn't going to let that go. No. There was only one answer to any question. Finish. "Get this body out of here. The others will know I mean business. They'll do what I tell them."

Mon pursed his lips and slapped his thighs with his hands. "We could have taken the doctors to your facility in Iran."

"You know that wouldn't work. We surely would have been found out, the products confiscated, and we would receive nothing." Abdi's frustrations came through in his wavering voice, his shaky movements and he knew it. "And if things turned sour, the Humanzees would be used against us. No. That would not work." Mon was Abdi's best friend, had been with him from the beginning, was a smart and trustworthy man, but there was no listening to his council now. It was too late. Finish. Finish. That's all Abdi could think. Just one more mass insemination. After speaking with his friend, Abdi motioned for him to go.

Mon got up from his usual chair where he witnessed killing after killing without commenting. He hesitated at the door as though he were going to say something, but then walked out and closed the door behind him.

Abdi left the room a few minutes after Mon. He made the short walk down the hallway. Guards stood in corner areas in the hall, outside most rooms he passed, and at the base of the stairs. Two men passed him on the stairs, heading up to remove the body from the upstairs office. The old farmhouse floors creaked as he walked. He found Mon in the large living room sitting on a leather settee.

Mon motioned toward the far end of the settee for Abdi to sit with him. A guard stood with his back against the wall in a far corner. The guard's eyes did not move. Abdi sat down and crossed his legs. Mon said nothing for a few minutes.

"You have a plan?" Abdi questioned.

"There is only one, but with many pieces."

"I will not take the doctors to Iran. Everything would fall apart."

"No. That has been established. I would not ask you to do something you feel so strongly you should not do." Mon leaned forward and placed his elbows on his knees, his hands out. He stared at the carpet. "We have twenty girls coming in two days. I will make it the last. My source will not be happy."

"We should have the doctors here, both of them. Bring all their equipment. They can do everything in the converted barn. We don't have to wait for sterilization, for prepping," he waved his hand in the air, "or whatever it is they suggest. Just do the job, even if it doesn't take every time. We've had so many failures thus far, a few more won't matter. The order was a delivery of a few a year. We've already surpassed that." He glanced away from Mon, then back at him again. "We should never have kept those beasts in Shirazi's clinic for experimentation. We should have shipped them long ago. They are healthy, our healthiest. All the others will be the same. Already the others are doing well."

"That is too late. We can't move them, not now," Mon said. They both knew what Mon meant. It would be a loss. Dr. Shirazi wouldn't be happy about it. He was promised research specimens. "You must be gone," Mon said without looking at Abdi. "There are too many people coming and going from this place. You must find another place or leave this country."

"You will take care of things?" Abdi both liked and disliked the thought of Mon taking over. Part of him trusted Mon completely, but there was also a spark of doubt that Mon might take the money and never return. "Why would you do that?"

Mon shook his head. "I will set everything in motion, and then I'll leave as well."

Abdi's heart raced and he stood. That answered the question of Mon's loyalty. "We can't be sure it will get done if we both leave." He pointed to the guard in the corner. "These men are not soldiers. You've seen how stupid they act when left on their own. They would fumble everything. And without the fear of retribution…"

"Then I'll stay," Mon said. "I have to be here to take delivery of the girls anyway."

Abdi grinned at his old friend. He didn't have to say anything. "If Clarkson would have only trained one of our doctors."

"But he didn't." Mon stood now and walked in a small circle around the couch. "But it doesn't mean he won't eventually train someone. After all, we bargained and he won. We gave our word. But his wife is pregnant now. That was his wish."

"We don't need him?" Abdi's grin grew. "After the final inseminations? That means our original bargain is over. We get to start fresh with a new opportunity."

Mon laughed. "We have a new bargaining chip. Perhaps we go to Turkey and hide out. Clarkson and Shirazi could go with us. We could prolong our commitment. It would be worth millions more. There are other countries, other factions that might need what we can deliver." He appeared happy with the possibilities.

"You want to maintain your connections, order more girls?" Abdi asked.

"We'll wait, move around for a few months, then choose where to start again. I'll maintain my contacts, with promises that I plan to keep. They'll understand." He scratched his chin. "Turkey is a good idea. We might continue there."

"You are brilliant, my friend. You have the plans. You always have." Abdi nodded. It meant that whatever Mon wanted to happen would happen. "I will go whenever you say."

"Then you leave tonight," Mon said.

CHAPTER 21

Dr. Clarkson sat behind the desk with his head lowered into his hands as though worried. His eyes widened when Ten and Maria walked into the office. Within a few moments, he appeared to be back to his normal self. "Who let you in here?"

"Not important. You're in trouble," Ten said. "So it's a good thing you're here."

Dr. Clarkson put his palms on the desk and leaned back. "Don't you think we know that?" Clarkson appeared more disgusted than angry or worried now, and Ten could understand why.

Things had gotten complicated toward the end. Clarkson probably hadn't even thought that far ahead. He'd wanted his son back, which Ten understood, but he had cleared every other possibility out of his head while aiming for that one thing. Now that Karla was pregnant and ISTI knew what Clarkson was up to, his alternatives shrunk to a miniscule number.

"Maybe you know, but to what extent do you think your supporters will stick behind you?"

Clarkson just stared at them. "Who are you anyway? You come to my office, you charge in here as though you own the place. What is it you want? The science? My research? Are you wanting control of the animals? What?"

"We're independent contractors, just like you," Ten said. He stepped closer to the desk where Clarkson sat.

Clarkson pushed the chair back as though trying to get away, but there was nowhere to go but to the wall. "We have this under control," he said rather unconvincingly.

"No, you don't," Maria said.

"They need us. We made sure of that."

"Tides shift," Ten said. He tapped the desktop. "As soon as they think they don't need you, you're gone. I hope you know that. I've seen this happen before."

Clarkson raised his eyebrows. "Experience?"

"Direct experience." With a quick glance toward Maria, Ten added, "Both of us."

"They're not shifting this time. I don't know what you went through, but I do know what I'm able to do…" He stopped talking and stared at Ten then at Maria.

"You're not so sure," Ten said. "Do you know what they promised their clients? Would you know when they're finished delivering?" With a wave of his hand, he said, "You were too focused on recreating your son." Ten knew it was a harsh attack, but he wanted Clarkson to break out of his stupidity and see what he'd gotten himself into.

Maria must have seen Clarkson hesitate, because she jumped right in with her own agenda. Ten felt rather proud that she knew when to ask the question. "Where do the girls come from?" she asked directly.

But it didn't work. Clarkson scoffed at her. "That's what you're worried about? You're not concerned that these people are creating an army of Humanzees? Ground fighters like nothing else ever before possible."

Ten felt that he was prouder of his accomplishments than he should be. By the look of the boy Humanzees he and Maria had seen, they were as much like scared children than warriors. Not that it couldn't change with the right training, but inside the Humanzees were, after all, human.

"You're not concerned about the girls?" Maria asked. "What kind of man are you? You'll work your ass off to reproduce what you lost, but you care nothing for the lost lives of others?"

He lowered his eyes.

"You got what you want," Maria said, disgusted. "That's all that matters. You don't care about where the Humanzees are sent off to. You don't care about the young girls these monsters are using." She rushed to the side of the desk, leaned close to Clarkson, and slapped him across the face. "Karla is pregnant, and this is the type of father you're going to be? No compassion for others? You don't deserve—"

Ten grabbed her arm and gently pulled her away. "Not now, Maria, not now."

Dr. Shirazi opened the door and his eyes went wide. "You two again."

"You bet your damned ass it is," Ten said. He removed his Glock and pointed it. "Over here with your buddy."

Shirazi raised his hands about chest high. "You don't need that. We'll listen. We want your help." He sounded serious.

Ten closed the door and wiggled the end of his pistol toward a chair near the other wall. "Pull that next to Clarkson and have a seat."

As soon as Shirazi sat, Clarkson looked at him and said, "Speak for yourself. I don't need their help."

Shirazi glanced at his partner in crime, then locked eyes with Ten. "He only wanted one thing." He turned his head toward Maria. "You know what it was. And now he has it. His wife is pregnant. I think they'll try to reach a new agreement with him." He looked distraught and lowered his eyes. He talked directly to Clarkson. "You know that for my part in this they could easily, and with little effort, find someone else to duplicate everything I did. I was protected by your deal." Shirazi's hands shook as he spoke. Like a frightened deer, his eyes couldn't stay on one person for long before he glanced toward the next person and the next. "With that deal over, they don't need me. Even if they still need you." He stopped talking to Clarkson and addressed Ten. "And when they have enough of what they want, they won't need him."

"We were just discussing that," Ten said.

Clarkson waved a hand to dismiss Shirazi's announcement. "They are greedy. They will always want more. More Humanzees. More money. I grew up knowing that the rich have no boundaries when it comes to greed."

"That's enough talk," Ten said. He held his gun up in the air for display and to get Clarkson and Shirazi's attention, then tucked it behind him and back into his waistband. "We need a plan, and quick."

Shirazi lowered his hands once Ten put away his gun.

Ten jerked his head toward Clarkson and then looked at Maria, giving her room to question him.

"Where do you perform the inseminations?" Maria asked immediately.

"Good question," Ten said. "We can stop that at the least."

"Different places," Shirazi said.

"We saw the Humanzees…" Ten motioned toward the rear of the building.

Shirazi shook his head. "Those are specimens they promised me. Early attempts didn't make it, then they lived a few years. I was trying to find out why." He looked at Dr. Clarkson. "With some help."

Clarkson nodded. "I made some adjustments and it seems to have worked."

"No degeneration of the cells, no breakdown—"

Clarkson put his hand on Shirazi's knee to stop him from talking. He nodded toward Maria.

"It doesn't matter," she said. "Whatever you did worked. The Humanzees will live. I don't know what we'll do with them, how smart they are, or what this means to science— well, maybe I do—but it's done. Now we have to save those girls. We have to stop this cruel and horrible exploitation of innocent lives."

"Moral grounds," Clarkson said. He slapped his own knee. "That's what's wrong with you. You may not like what I'm doing, but I don't limit my science or my life like you do," he said directly to Ten. "My son was taken from me and my wife, and that was not moral."

He looked sad to Ten, a sadness that penetrated more deeply than life itself. A sadness Ten understood and had gone through. Something had been taken from him and he processed it with anger. For a moment, Ten knew that his own processing channeled through guilt. What was the difference between them? He took a deep breath. "I don't care about your reasoning." He talked to himself as much as to Clarkson. "We're going to stop this. All of it. Your expertise should be used for your own country, not theirs, not for money."

Clarkson stared at Ten for the second time, as though his look alone would transfer his anger, his hatred, his explanation. But Ten didn't connect with him at all. He saw only a mixed-up man who grieved for the loss of his son and took creation into his own hands. The right idea for the wrong reasons? Or the wrong idea for the right reasons? Ten broke eye contact with Clarkson and smiled at Maria.

She turned to Shirazi. "When are you doing the next insemination? And where?"

"I don't know. They tell me when and where. I don't know until I get the call."

"But it's not here; at least, not every time," she said.

His face twitched, but he didn't answer.

"He gets the call a day or so after I get the call," Clarkson said, drawing the attention from his friend. "I have to prepare everything on my end. That's my talent."

He appeared a bit cocky to Ten, but Ten also read through the statement. "They've already called."

As soon as he said that, Shirazi's eyes jerked toward a package on his desk.

Ten reached for it but laid his hand on top of it lightly instead of picking it up. He didn't want to disturb whatever was sealed inside. "What about going through MCL?"

"I think they're running scared. They must know about you, so you're not safe," Clarkson said.

"And you don't give a shit about that," Maria said.

"Your job. You must have skills. That is not my concern," Clarkson said.

"I don't know what Karla sees in you," Maria said. She put her hand on Ten's arm and his attention shifted to her. "That means that Shirazi will most likely get that call today."

Ten gave her his best "I'm not scared" look while the bile in his stomach increased into an acidic mess. "We'll wait for that call. In the meantime, call…" he looked at the two men and said, "you know who to call. Maria, I want you out of harm's reach. You can't be here."

She shook her head slowly and let her eyes narrow. "You haven't been listening. I'm in on this to the end. I don't care what happens."

"But I do," he said.

Shirazi interrupted their dispute. "I have patients," he said. "I have work to do. It would only alert them…"

"He's right," Ten said. "It should be business as usual." To Clarkson, he said, "Is this your last shipment? Do you have to be concerned about Karla?"

His demeanor switched from cocky to concern, but Ten couldn't tell if it was love or fear that created it. From all outward signs, something had died inside Dr. Clarkson. He appeared to be going through the motions and that was all. But any thread that led back to his son still had an effect on him. That one thing. It was sad to see.

"Call her and have her meet you here."

Clarkson's face turned to curiosity. "You two can't protect us." The statement was a fact, not even Clarkson's voice indicated any possibility that it was untrue.

"Get her here," Ten said. "We'll worry about the rest of it. As for you," he said to Shirazi, "get to work. When they call, you relay that information to one of us. Got it?"

Shirazi nodded. "Another thing…"

"I don't need another thing, but go ahead," Ten said.

"People who work for them, whoever they are, join us in the afternoon to study the Humanzees. They will know something is up if you are here."

"We're not leaving," Ten said. "Not until you get that phone call. Maybe we'll be lucky and it'll happen before they arrive. For now, you service your customers."

Ten and Maria stepped aside so Shirazi could leave.

"You trust him?" Clarkson asked.

"Yes." Ten didn't want anyone to question his commitment to what he said.

"So, what about me?" Clarkson asked.

"You call Karla and get her over here."

"Won't she be in worse danger? It's just the two of you. Unless you have others spying on the building. You know, these people have killed before. I've heard—"

"Don't care what you've heard," Ten said. "This is how it's going down." He removed his cell phone from his shirt pocket and held it toward Clarkson.

"I don't remember the number." He pulled his own phone from his pocket and made the call. It was short, not as sweet as Ten would have thought, and then over. "She'll be here in an hour."

Chapter 22

"One of us could have stayed," Maria said. "Jacob's men were assigned to watch the place. If you wanted me safe…"

Ten drove as usual, but his mind was occupied, and he didn't answer right away. The statement had to sink in. "Better this way," he said. "Honestly, you just might be safer with me than with them. Clarkson and Shirazi are the main scientists on this gig. Karla is a tool for whoever is behind this to use against her husband. I'm sorry to say that she might be a tool for him to get his son back too."

She didn't agree and made that known. "She wouldn't let this happen if it wasn't what she wanted too. Trust me. A woman's body is her own. She wouldn't do this."

"Maybe if she loved him enough, she'd do it. Even if he turned into a total ass."

"And how did you come to that conclusion?" Ten continued to drive. She stared at him from the passenger seat. "You're not going to stop worrying about me, are you? I can take care of myself."

"We would both be in danger if we were caught there. Surveillance is the best way. We might gain information easier that way. Having us there would only increase the possibility for confrontation. I know Jacob said he'd have us watched too, but I don't know what the hell that means. Is there a cavalry he can send in or are there two people sitting in a van with binoculars like I'm sure he has at the clinic? I'm not taking any chances for either one of us."

"So…"

"He got the call and we know the location. We know the time… tomorrow evening, after hours for Dr. Shirazi. We don't need to do anything more. We stop here. It's someone else's problem."

"I'm going," she said.

"What do you mean you're going? What in the world can you do to help? Let Jacob take care of it. That's his job. Twenty girls. They're going to have all kinds of protection and the main people won't be there anyway. I guarantee it. In fact, if Jacob does what he says he can do, there won't be any girls that even get to the location."

She grinned at him. Her curly hair and wide eyes added to the look of pleasure.

"What?"

"You haven't called Jacob to tell him you're out. You're still considering what to do. You're playing with ideas in your head. I can tell. And you're getting close to a plan, aren't you?"

He couldn't help but smile back at her. She knew him better than he thought. "I should be seeing you as the psychologist instead of this Carol Olmstead woman. What's she capable of that you can't intuit?"

She laughed. "Oh, she's much better at this than I am. She has training."

"That's a scary thought, that she needs special training to deal with me."

"Oh, you know that's true. Besides, she's a psychiatrist, not a psychologist."

"The big guns," Ten said.

"So what is it? What do we do?" Maria wanted to know.

"The next thing we do is alert Jacob that the girls are already in the country and hand over the location of the drop-off so he can post people all around. There must be some trail he can follow to find out how the girls got into the country, but that's not important at the moment. But then, none of this has anything to do with catching who's really bringing the girls through. Or who's apprehending them, which would have to include international alliances, I'm sure."

"You're right, that's an international situation that I'm sure we're going to get to work on. We'll have to rely on Jacob; and if not him and his team at ISTI, then someone higher up. It's out of our hands at this point. But if we can catch them at the handoff, perhaps it will give us a thread, even a small one, that stretches in each direction." Maria looked serious about the predicament. "Twenty girls," she said, "that's not easy to hide."

"Sure it is: soccer team, baseball team. In this case, a school trip?"

"From a militarized zone?"

He put two and two together in his head. He wasn't an expert but knew enough: there were ways to hide what you were doing. "Who knows how many handoffs there were before they got into position for this delivery. They could have entered and exited several countries on their way to the US. It might not be as easy as you'd hoped. These people could bring the girls in two at a time for all we know."

Houses rushed by out her side window as they drove. "You're probably right." Now it was Maria's turn to be preoccupied with her own thoughts. Ten realized she was thinking of a plan as well, and probably would come up with a better one than his. She was so much smarter than he was and he knew it. When she swung back around, she shook her head. "We stop it here!" She poked a finger into the dashboard. "If that's all we have, then we stop it wherever we can. We tell Jacob what we know. We let him do his damned research, but we go there, and we stop them no matter what he says, no matter what the consequences." She then used the same finger to poke Ten's arm. She looked as though she was about to cry. She meant to save those girls and he knew it, even if he didn't know why she was so passionate about it. "*We* stop them. I don't want to rely on anyone else. We're going to be at that location tomorrow night."

Ten felt concern for how adamant Maria expressed herself about the situation. The thought crossed his mind that perhaps she had been raped or abused as a young girl and couldn't fathom that happening to anyone else; perhaps she felt for anyone in a war zone that was taken advantage of. He didn't know what the issue was, but he did know what the reaction was through Maria. She was serious. He finally understood that no matter how much he wanted to protect her, no matter how much he didn't want her involved, she was staying. There was absolutely nothing he could do about it. But it didn't stop him from worrying for both their sakes.

"Okay," he said. "We go back to the apartment and get some rest. We lay low for the rest of tonight and tomorrow, until tomorrow evening. We turn in everything we know. If Jacob says to let it alone, we consider it." He looked over at her, knowing she wasn't about to consider it at all. "And then we make a decision."

"No, we don't," she said, much more calm than only a moment ago.

Ten recognized the finality of the statement. Just what he expected. She didn't have to yell or poke anything; she meant it. A shot of anxiety shot through him the moment she asserted herself. He feared for her safety. Twenty girls would be guarded well. He didn't mind dying for the cause, but he wouldn't be able to bear it if anything happened to her. She was under his care. They should never have pulled together for this job in the first place. He didn't need the partnership. They never really got into the medical specifics anyway. He didn't need an interpreter. He didn't want her there. He just didn't. "Fine, but we bring Jacob in. I'm sure he'll stop the delivery before we have to get overly involved."

"As soon as he does, those girls will need someone to talk with, and I'm there. So we aim for the farmhouse where they're going to do the inseminations, but once we hear from Jacob that he has the girls, we go wherever he has them instead. They're going to need someone like me. They're going to need a woman."

"I want Jacob to know that. I also want backup for us if we're going to that farmhouse to make a visit."

"It doesn't matter, Ten. The guards will most likely be with the girls, not at the farm."

Although the weather was beautiful, Ten hardly noticed until they were back at the apartment complex and he was out of the car. On the short walk toward the front of their building, he glanced around the best he could to see if he saw their guards. Nothing. Either they were very clever and hid well, or they weren't there. Since this wasn't official business, Ten was already surprised at the number of people Jacob had hanging around. They took the stairs and wandered down the hall and into the apartment. No sooner did they arrive then the landline rang. Ten picked up the phone. "Yeah?"

"We're going to send up your dinner right away. You can debrief with the agent who delivers it." The phone clicked off. So they were followed.

The news made Ten feel protected, but the fact he didn't notice them made him feel vulnerable. What if they were followed by other people not out to protect them? "Sure thing," he said before dropping the phone into its cradle. He knew no one was there to hear him, but he said it anyway. "These guys are efficient," he said.

"Why? Who was that? Jacob?"

"No. They're sending up dinner and someone to debrief us."

"They must know we're here," she said.

Ten walked over to the door, opened it, and bent down to look into the lock. "Must be a nano-switch of some kind." He examined the door jam, ran his fingers along the door, then realized it could be the welcome mat, and with one foot tapped on it a few times. "Or pressure on the mat. They wouldn't have to see us if they were just monitoring the apartment."

"Leave it alone. You don't have to search for it. It could just be that they have someone in the parking lot who saw us."

He shrugged. "Maybe, but I didn't see anyone."

She didn't comment. "One thing," she said after he put down his backpack and removed the gun from his pants.

"What's that?"

"Just because we're going to be busy tomorrow night doesn't mean you have an excuse to miss your appointment with Carol tomorrow morning."

The elevator dinged at the end of the hall and he saw an agent with a bag of takeout walking toward him. He smiled at Maria. "Relentless."

"You know it."

"Well, we'll see where we stand soon."

While the two of them ate at the small kitchen counter, the agent set up a tape recorder, but also took notes on a small notepad while they debriefed. There wasn't much to tell. They had relayed most of the information to Jacob.

"This Clarkson guy sounds pretty ruthless and cold," the agent said. He had introduced himself as Agent Browne.

"Not ruthless, apathetic," Ten said. "It doesn't seem to register to him that other people matter in this world. Not even young girls kidnapped."

"Too bad."

"Yeah, because other people do matter."

"Let me get back to the home office and I'll let you know what they say if I'm allowed to," Agent Browne said.

"If you're allowed?"

He nodded politely. "That's what I said. None of us knows the whole story. That's what keeps us safe."

"Sometimes it just keeps you in the dark." Ten shook his head, then followed Agent Browne to the door. "You'll call tonight?"

"Probably in less than an hour," he said.

When the call came in, Maria was sitting on the couch in her pajamas and Ten was in his room doing pushups. He needed to move. Being cooped up in the car and the office at the clinic and not being able to walk around made his muscles ache.

Maria answered the phone and talked for a few minutes, then hung up. Ten heard her as she walked in her bare feet to his bedroom doorway. "That was the call."

"And?" He slid his legs under him and remained sitting on the floor. He still wore his jeans, the same ones he had on all day. He had taken off his outer shirt, though, and sat in his t-shirt, no shoes or socks. He knew she could see some of the cuts he'd administered but didn't try to hide them. She knew about it, so what would matter?

"They're going to research every large group of girls coming into the country from any foreign country on a recent flight. At least that. He said they'd figure it out and I believe him."

"Me too, eventually. As for tomorrow night, though, they may be driving in from New Jersey," he said. "How do we know these girls haven't been in this country for months? Even years? How do we know they haven't had menial jobs for a while and are taking a bus? What the hell?"

"Trust Jacob. He knows what he's doing."

"Research. You know what that means."

"They may not be able to stop the girls from arriving. I know. I asked about that. I was told he'd take care of it from there. He knows the final location. He'll stop this one way or another. He promised."

<h1 style="text-align:center">CHAPTER 23</h1>

Maria stood in the doorway, staring at Ten. He knew what she was thinking but didn't want to say it. He wanted Jacob to intercept the delivery of the girls and all those people connected to them. He wanted to be done with the two doctors, the Humanzees, the whole project. He didn't feel as strongly about the potential dangers of a Humanzees army as Jacob. He felt for the girls, though perhaps not as deeply and passionately as Maria. Neither of those facts mattered as much as the third. Most of all, he wanted Maria to be safe. Looking at her while she stared at him was a reminder of what he knew and how different that was from what he wished. Somewhere deep inside, he had already agreed. He knew. She wasn't letting this go and he'd be there beside her.

"I want to be there when the delivery takes place." She gestured with her palms up as though there were nothing she could do about the decision, like it wasn't up to her what she wanted.

He said, "I don't like it. You should stay here. I can do this. Actually, Jacob can do this, and should do this. Dammit!" His frustration leaked through. "Neither of us should have to go. We did our part. We brought all of this together." Even as he tried to rationalize the events, he could see her conviction. "But if one of us has to go, it should be me. Not you."

"Well, you're not going alone," she said.

"Most likely it won't get that far. It won't matter. The girls will be found and rescued by Jacob's team long before they reach the house where the inseminations are to take place," he said.

"Then there is no danger either way. Nothing to worry about."

He let out a long breath, then waited a moment for her to say something else. When she didn't, he said, "I don't like it."

"We've established that. You don't have to." She left the doorway, the empty space, hollow without her standing there.

It was going to be a long night.

Once he relaxed, Ten walked down the hall to Maria's bedroom and the door was closed. He reached up to knock but changed his mind. She had said her piece, maybe he should leave her alone. They both needed sleep.

He took a quick shower and put on a pair of shorts for bed. After turning out the light, he lay awake for a long time. He slept on his back and sometimes when he couldn't sleep, he stared at the ceiling and used it as a movie screen where his past played out before him. Depressing but familiar.

He had an urge to cut his shoulder, but he wasn't in his own apartment. He wasn't alone. If Maria caught him… Every time he reached to scratch at his healing skin, he thought about how it would feel for his paring knife to penetrate ever so slightly, how the blood would look, and how, for a moment, he would actually *feel* something other than sadness. A spark of survival might rise up inside him. Something always stopped him from continuing. A short two- or three-inch cut, not very deep, was enough. He'd stop there. He wasn't looking forward to talking with the psychiatrist the next day, but he had promised Maria and wasn't about to break that promise just yet.

Ten eventually fell asleep for a few hours and awoke early, ran through a series of pushups and sit-ups, then stretches. After another quick shower, he brushed his teeth, shaved, combed his hair, and dressed for the day. When he walked into the kitchen, Maria stood at the counter with a coffee cup between her hands. Still in her pajamas, her curly hair poked in all directions. She wore no makeup and still looked good.

When she was with Ben, before he died, she looked beautiful. They were a happy couple, just as he and Amy were. He never looked at Maria in any other way but as a friend. That morning she was a good-looking friend.

"Good morning." Her voice sounded deeper than usual, as though she were climbing out of a deep and dusty pit. She cleared her throat. "Sleep well?" She was out of the pit now, and sounded closer to normal, still tired.

"Not really," Ten said. "Look—"

"Don't even say it. You're worried that if something happened to me, your"—she pointed at his shoulder, even though he had a long-sleeved shirt on this morning—"affliction would get worse."

"I don't want anyone else to get hurt because of what I choose to do. My anger can get the best of me."

"I was in on this before you were. Long before. So let's drop it. There's nothing more to discuss."

He poured himself a cup of coffee and put some creamer in it. "You win. It's dropped." It wasn't over for him though. He planned to do everything he could to keep her safe, and that wasn't going to change no matter what she said or did, and no matter what Jacob had planned.

Midmorning, just before Ten headed for the door to go to his appointment, the phone rang. He picked it up and listened as someone, he suspected Agent Browne by the man's voice, told him that Jacob had several teams working on other projects still, and there'd be a limited number of agents available. "Nonetheless," Browne said, "we expect to be able to stop the delivery with no problem and won't be needing your or Maria's help."

"How?" Ten asked. "Do you know where the girls are coming from?"

"Not yet, but that's not your concern. I'm to deliver this message. Jacob said you were eager to get out and he's giving you that option now."

"Does 'not yet' mean no, because that's what I suspect it means."

"We're on top of it. You can lay low tonight. Even if we can't stop the delivery before it arrives, we know where to go. We know the final destination. We can handle this. Got that?"

Ten didn't like his tone. "Yeah, I 'got that.'" He hung up.

Maria wore a bathrobe and stood at the doorway to the kitchen. Her hair lay flat along her head. "You don't look happy. What'd they want?"

"Jacob's got people on the job. We don't have to be there. That was Agent Browne relaying the message from Jacob, or so he said."

"If that's true, you don't look as happy as you should be." She smiled and winked. "You're pretty easy to read, you know. I don't care what you choose to think." She brushed her hands through her hair. "I'm going to be there tonight." She turned away and walked toward her bedroom.

"Jacob said he's got it," Ten said.

"Don't care. We can talk about it when you get back. Tell Carol I said hello."

Ten left the apartment and waved when he exited the building. He had no idea where his followers were but wanted to acknowledge to them that he knew they were there. And if he were wrong about that, the wave would mean nothing. The drive to Dr. Olmstead's office was easy at that time of day, about a ten-minute drive, which gave him time to think about what he might say, what information he might wish to give up and what he wouldn't tell her.

There was no receptionist in the office, so he sat in a leather chair and flipped through *Outdoor* magazine while he waited. In a few minutes, the door to her office opened. A young woman of about twenty-three—maybe five foot four, brown hair, slender body, average looks, and brown eyes—came through the door. She glanced at Ten, turned her head back into the office, probably to address Dr. Olmstead and said, "Thank you, Carol. I feel better already." Ten hoped he'd feel better in an hour as well, but he wasn't sure what that would be like anymore.

Dr. Olmstead spoke from deep inside the office. "I'll see you in a month, then." She walked to the door and looked directly at Ten. "You must be Mr. Nesbit." Ten nodded. "I'll be with you in just a moment." She gave him a quick smile and folded back into her office as though unable to leave. She closed the door. After another five minutes, she opened the door again, held the knob, and asked him to enter.

Ten stood and walked past her. She dressed well, a dark skirt, light blue blouse, green earrings to match her eyes. Light brown hair, almost blonde in some areas, even though there was little sun in her office. There was only one window to the side, which let in the bulk of the light in the office. She closed the door, still standing close to him since he stopped walking once inside. She held out her hand. "It's a pleasure to meet you."

"All mine," Ten said. Her hand felt soft inside his. She had a secure grip, but not exactly firm. She appeared genuine, with a kind demeanor.

She motioned toward a chair to one side in front of her desk that sat slightly cocked, then sat in her own chair behind the desk. A folder lay in front of her, opened and flat. She flipped through a few sheets as though she'd been working with him for a long time. He wondered where the notes had come from.

"Maria has talked about you often. You two went through a harrowing experience. You both lost someone you loved."

Was she giving him the short version of his life for some reason? There was no need. He lived the long version and remembered it perfectly, maybe too perfectly.

He leaned forward and when she paused for a breath, he said, "We aren't the same person. We don't handle events the same way." His stomach tightened. The plan was not to be combative, but the words came out anyway.

She sat back in her chair. "I realize that. No two people do." She looked at him for a long thirty seconds. "How do you feel about being here?"

"Coerced."

"I'm sure Maria meant well."

"I know she did."

"Perhaps you aren't ready to see someone," she said.

"That's what I said." He eased back into his chair. "But I promised her."

"Then you're committed?"

He sensed a battle going on inside himself and didn't know how to resolve it. The answer to her question was yes and no. He took a breath. He needed an answer. Ten lowered his eyes and felt his chest contract; his shoulder muscles tightened. He became aware of his self-inflicted wounds and wanted to scratch his shoulder. He was sure Maria told the doctor about that too, but he didn't need to point to it right away. So he let the itch annoy him. When he looked up, Dr. Olmstead hadn't moved, not even her eyebrows. She looked calm, and somehow that calmed him too. "I'm committed."

"This might get ugly," she said. "If you stay."

"I understand." He hesitated. "It's ugly now."

"I have a few more questions before we start. It's like an entry questionnaire, so it's pretty simple and fairly non-personal."

"I'm ready, Doctor—"

She closed the folder and smiled. "Carol. Doctor keeps us separated."

"Carol it is."

"How do you feel about what happened before? What I mean is, are you angry, sad, resolved?" Her elbows were on her desk and the fingers of both hands met. She let her fingers bounce as though they were a ticking clock waiting for him to answer within an allotted time.

He didn't like to be pressured. He took his time, took a deep breath, then answered. "Devastated." He held back his raging emotions, held back tears.

"Your wife was pregnant with your first child. I can see how you'd feel." She lowered her hands onto the desk and leaned forward. "I can see it's upsetting. We can come back to that later." He nodded, nothing more. "You've been cutting yourself, Maria tells me." She smiled. "She told me you knew that I knew."

"She's been honest with me from the start."

"Does that help?"

"Sometimes," he said.

"Can you tell me about your life before all this began? Not from childhood, but perhaps from when you started your job."

Ten relaxed briefly and wondered if her first questions were to get him to open up the second she eased up on him. It didn't matter. At the moment, it gave him a reason to provide her some background about him and Amy. Their life together. He took the opportunity and spent the next fifty minutes explaining to her how perfect his life had become, how perfect it was until recently.

After the appointment, Ten called Maria's phone to let her know he completed their deal… and that he had made a second appointment.

She didn't answer. He left a message.

Chapter 24

He hit redial on his phone several times while driving back to the apartment. He continued to get her voicemail. He tried Jacob, but the call never went through. On his fifth try, logic kicked in. First, he scanned the road ahead and to either side of him, glanced in his rearview mirror. Was he being followed? Watched? He searched the inside of the car for his backpack. Did he have his gun? No. Had he left everything at the apartment? Had Maria distracted him? Why didn't he remember to bring his backpack? He knew the answer. He didn't expect any trouble. He was just going to his appointment, that was all.

He took a few deep breaths and let them out long and slow. His head cleared. His memory returned, even though he had been preoccupied the first part of his trip. Was it the second car behind him that had turned the last time he turned and was behind him for a short while? At his last turn, another car slipped between them, but the second car was riding close. While peering into his mirror, he noticed how that car drove closer to the center of the road than the car directly behind him. When had they started to follow him? And when would they make their attack?

Ten was pissed he had not thought to bring his backpack with his Glock 19. He leaned and opened the glove compartment, but nothing but paperwork filled the space. It was worth a try. At a stop sign, he turned left instead of right. He didn't even know why.

He sped up and made a quick right, then another right to correct his seemingly evasive turn, hoping they had not seen the second right. They weren't behind him at the moment. Another stop sign sat up ahead and he planned to run it if he could see far enough to either side to do it safely. No sense in putting anyone else's life in danger, but he needed to ditch them so he could get back to the apartment, where he was safe.

A narrow alley sat ahead to his right. Before he could adjust his speed, a car rushed from behind a bush and rammed into the side of his SUV, shoving it to the opposite side of the road. Thank God no one sat in the passenger seat.

It was all happening so quickly. His adrenaline set in, giving him the extra boost he needed. He rammed the door open with his shoulder and leaped from the car. The moment he hit the ground, he flattened onto the pavement so he could see under the SUV to the other side. Two men jumped from the car that smashed into him and began to walk carefully around his car. He rolled under the SUV and crawled forward on his knees and elbows as best he could along the ground. One man stopped at the left front corner of the SUV, the other man right behind him. Ten reached out, grabbed the second man's leg, twisted and yanked as hard as he could. He heard a snap and felt the reverberation through his grip on the man's ankle. Something broke. Most likely the tibia.

The man yelled, dropped to the ground, and reached for his leg, hitting his head on the grill. He fell flat. Knocked out. The other man jumped back. Ten didn't know if he had a gun or not, but decided to roll out from under the SUV anyway. He leaped up. The first man, still looking at his buddy, reacted with surprise to see Ten standing so close to him. His surprise lasted long enough for Ten to leap over the hood and knock the pistol from the man's hand using his elbow. At such closeness, Ten was able to slam his two fists to either side of the man's face. He then shoved the man backward, lost his own balance, and fell on top of the man. The man swung and hit Ten in the shoulder, but not with much force. He brought his knees up and arms in to shove Ten from him. Once Ten rolled off, the man kicked out toward Ten while still lying on the ground. He wasn't a very effective fighter. He started to get up and hit Ten in the shoulder a second time.

No problem.

Ten scrambled for the dropped pistol and the other man dove on top of him. He was a big man and Ten tightened his body to protect himself from the impact. SLAM! Ten's forehead hit the pavement hard and bounced off. He scrunched his face up from the pain, took a quick breath, and lifted to his knees as quickly as he could. He pitched forward, knocking the pistol farther down the road. Another car had stopped, and the driver jumped out. He yelled back to his passenger to call the police.

The man on top of Ten wrapped an arm around his neck and began to squeeze. Ten brought one leg up in order to rise from the pavement again. In a crouched position, Ten reached back and grabbed the man's hair as close to the back of his neck as possible—and pulled with all his might.

The man screamed, pushed forward with his own legs to ease the pressure, and Ten folded into a curve and flipped the man over. On the ground, in front of him and upside down, Ten used a straight hand to drive into the man's neck, collapsing his esophagus. While the man choked, Ten scrambled for the pistol.

Ten thanked the men who had stopped for calling the police. "But I can't stay for this." He placed the dropped pistol on the hood of the other men's car, then opened the car door and yanked some wiring from under the car's dash. By the time the police arrived, he had tied both of his attackers up using the wire and had bent his license plate so it couldn't be read. The moment the police car stopped, Ten leaped into the driver's seat and squealed off in his SUV. He knew they'd call for backup, but he'd ditch the car a block or two over and steal one for the remainder of his trip. He had to get back to the apartment as fast as he could and didn't need a police escort.

While driving a tan 2014 Ford Focus toward the apartment building, he pulled over to let a police car, sirens blaring, pass him going the opposite direction. He reached up, after glancing into the rearview mirror and seeing blood on his forehead, to wipe his cut on his shirt sleeve. He barely remembered being slammed into the pavement. The cut looked worse than it felt.

He thought of his trip to Dr. Olmstead's office. The morning had started out so good. It sure turned quickly.

Luckily, his cell phone had remained in his shirt pocket. He had no idea how that happened except that it had a rubber case. He redialed Maria only to get her voicemail, then tried Jacob again. Someone answered and promised to patch him through, but the phone went dead after a few clicks and pops. The same as before. Jacob wasn't answering either or wasn't available. Not a good sign.

At the apartment building, Ten parked along the side, let the car run, and rushed close to the building, around the corner, and up to the front door. He went inside and ran toward the elevator, which he hoped would be faster than the stairs. It looked like blood on the floor as he stepped inside. Things were turning badly. The moment the door closed, he thought he should have taken the stairs. Too late.

At his floor, the elevator doors opened, and he instantly saw a body to his right. The hallway was empty. He kneeled down and checked for a pulse. There was one. He examined the body for bullet holes and found none. The man was only knocked out. Whoever came for Maria could still be there waiting for him to arrive too.

Ten rushed down the hall, bent over to create a smaller target. The door to the apartment stood open. He placed his back against the wall and scooted in. That's when he heard the scream. His ears perked. He instantly knew it wasn't from inside the apartment, so he ran to the nearest window overlooking the front parking lot. Two men hauled Maria toward a black Lincoln. Another man held the door open. Ten couldn't make it down there in time and he knew it. So he rushed into his room, found his Glock, and ran back to the window. They were pulling away.

Chapter 25

Before getting to the first landing, Ten swung around and went back upstairs, leaping two and three stairs at a time. As he burst through the door, he heard the man lying beside the elevator moan, low and guttural. Ten bent to one knee next to the man, who looked as though he was trying to get up. One arm reached toward Ten. "You okay?"

"I think so. Got hit from behind." He was coming to.

"They took Maria," Ten said.

The man shook his head. "Call the home office."

"Tried that." Ten slipped his arm under the man's shoulder to help him sit up. After a brief moment, the man took a deep breath and reached for Ten. The two of them stood together, holding onto each other for stabilization. "A lot of good it was moving us here. They came for us anyway."

"We're running lean right now. You have no idea."

"I could have if someone would talk with me," Ten said.

"Classified."

"Bullshit. Look what classified did now. Besides, what I'm doing is supposed to be classified. No one's supposed to know I'm working with ISTI, yet there are more ISTI people running around me than ever before. Who's Jacob trying to fool?" Ten held onto the man's arm and walked him down the hall and into the apartment. He helped the agent sit in a chair, then rushed into his temporary bedroom and scooped up his backpack. He doublechecked to be sure his spare magazine was inside. He doublechecked on the agent to be sure he was doing all right.

"I'm fine. Be back to normal in no time," he said. Pointing at Ten's backpack, he asked, "Where do you think you're going?"

"Don't know, but I'm going to find out where that Lincoln drove off to and intercept it." He held out his hand. "Keys. And to which car? I need something they won't recognize."

"My car," the man said, taking the keys from his pocket slowly, as though deliberating whether to hand them over or not. Ten snatched them from the man's hand as soon as he could. "It's the red Camry. You should know that we have guys outside."

Ten stopped at the doorway and smiled at him. "If they were still there, and conscious, they would have tried to save Maria." He shook his head in disgust. "Maybe at least some of you guys should be trained better."

"We're trained—"

Ten didn't wait for whatever the man said. He darted out the door and down the hall toward the stairs, leaping down several at a time, just as he had ascended them.

In the parking lot, he nabbed the agent's Camry and squealed from the parking lot. He had no idea in which direction to go, so he drove in the direction of the mansion where they were going to deliver the girls that night. That's the only place that came to mind quickly. He wasn't on the road more than ten minutes when his cell phone began to ring. He pulled it from his shirt pocket. "Yes?"

"I'm sorry."

"Jacob! Why the hell didn't you answer? Why didn't someone answer?"

"No time to explain. Besides, it's classified. The whole damned shitload of it."

"I've heard that way too often today. Look, while I was out, they came and took—"

"Maria, I know. Carson called it in after you left him at the apartment."

"Why did you move us if you couldn't actually protect us? It makes no sense."

"Knock it off, Ten. I figured *you'd* be with her all the time. Otherwise we could have left you in your separate places."

"I had an appointment. She made me promise to go. Besides, you never said to stick together."

"An appointment? Aren't you on a case? What the hell are you…" He trailed off. "Never mind."

"So you didn't have very many men watching over us? You assumed I'd be there. I get it."

"Three men were on duty. One was on break when it happened. And I don't want to hear it! Where do you think they're going with her?"

"No idea."

"Then where are you going?"

Ten wanted to throw the phone across the car and let it smash into the passenger window, but he held it to his ear. "Toward the place where they're taking the girls."

"Don't do that. I have that taken care of."

"Like protecting Maria?"

"Not fair. You were with her too."

"Don't throw this back in my face. I'm not even working for you. Neither of us are, yet you've shoved us into the middle of a huge mess."

"You walked into it," Jacob said.

Ten held his tongue. It wasn't his fault. No one told him to sit tight, to stay at the apartment, nothing. No guidelines, no suggestions, no help. "These guys are amateurs. You've got to know that. How can they just walk through your guys—even if there were only two of them—and you expect me to protect Maria? You're delusional, my friend."

"I'm trying to do a huge job with a small staff." Jacob sounded frustrated and depleted.

Ten held up his next jab at Jacob's inadequacies and got back on track with a simple question. "How can you help me now?"

"Let me take care of capturing the girls from those men. We know where they're headed tonight. Like I said before, we can intercept them."

"And if not?"

"Then we'll nab them during the delivery."

"Why not just wait until then? Wait until after the delivery and move in?"

"They'll be more heavily armed once the girls are delivered. They won't expect us to pull down a van or two on their way." Jacob sounded confident in his assessment.

"What about Maria? You know they're going to hold her hostage somehow. What do we do about her? In fact, what about the other girls who might be there? What about the Humanzees they must have in various stages, at various ages?"

There was a silence on the other end of the phone. "Okay. How about this: they don't know who the hell you are. So if you contact Clarkson and Shirazi and tell them you know their bosses have Maria, you can ask them what they want in exchange for her life."

"I can't deliver anything," Ten said. "I don't have any pull and you know it."

"I can deliver."

"Everyone knows we're involved in this, don't they? How could they not? You've already moved us, guarded us, and now you're saying you can back us up."

"They know about Maria and a partner, but don't know it's you. A few of the men do, others have no idea who you are or what you've done in the past. They don't know your connection to us."

"How lucky you are." Ten turned onto the highway but slowed the car. He stared as far ahead as he possibly could but saw no black Lincoln. There were black cars ahead, but nothing that big as far as he could tell. "What do you want me to do? I can't just sit on my ass and wait for you."

"Go back to the apartment and let us handle it."

"Again, not going to happen. Look, Jacob, I'm better trained than most of your guys out here. At least that's how it looks to me. I can at least fight. I'm your best bet. Let me help."

"I don't know."

"I'll head back to the apartment for a few hours. You'd better contact me with whatever information you have. Got that? I want to know if you've found out where Maria is. I want to know when and where your guys are going to intercept those deliveries. And I want to know if you fail so that I can be at that delivery location to nab her before anything happens."

Jacob's long slow breath meant he was giving in. In a low tone, he said, "I'll keep you informed the best I can."

"Good enough." Ten ended the call and finished his thought. "For now." At the next opportunity, he turned around to return the Camry to the parking lot.

Chapter 26

As he walked down the hall, Ten noticed that the door to the apartment stood open. The closer he got, the louder voices could be heard inside. He slowed but kept walking. Eventually the scene came into view. He saw three agents—the one he'd saved and two others—all dressed alike, with a fourth person, a nurse, who stood over one of the men, attending to a wound on his head.

"You're back," Carson, the agent from the hallway, said as Ten wandered in.

"You must be the Three Musketeers," Ten responded.

"Not funny," one of the other men said.

Ten entered the room completely and made his way closer to the group. "You're all lucky they didn't shoot you. In fact, I wonder why they didn't, unless they know you're government employees. Which I'm sure they do by now."

"Whoever they are, they're not very smart," the nurse said. When Ten looked at her, she added, "None of them were knocked out in the same way." She shrugged. "A trained Navy Seal, any trained attacker, in fact, would have known how best to do this."

"I take it none of you saw any of the men who hit you." None of them met Ten's gaze, indicating they saw nothing, just as he had suggested.

Agent Carson moved forward in his chair and raised his head to stare directly at Ten. "Enough of your sarcasm. Are you here to help us do this or not?"

It was Ten's turn not to say anything.

"Good. Since you're back, I take it you didn't find the kidnappers?" he said, repeating Ten's words and tone, which sent Ten's blood pressure up.

There was no reason for Ten to argue. He had delivered the sarcasm first, so Carson was justified. Ten already felt accused by Jacob for leaving Maria alone, even though these three guys were stationed there specifically to protect them both. There wasn't anything he could do if he didn't know Jacob's reason for putting the two of them together. He shook his head. "Jacob called and asked me to back off," Ten responded before walking toward his bedroom.

"Why do you think that was?" the agent asked after him.

Ten stopped for a moment. "He said he had it handled." Then Ten changed his mind and walked down the hall toward Maria's bedroom.

"No struggle," the first agent yelled after him.

Ten wandered back into the room. "I heard her scream."

"Reaction," the man sitting below the nurse said. "If someone shoved her, pulled her hair, anything like that, her scream may have been a reaction, involuntary."

"You know this?"

"I do." The agent didn't offer an explanation.

The nurse patted the man's shoulder and he got up from in front of her and went over to sit on the couch. "You're next," she said to Ten. When he didn't react right away, she pointed toward his forehead. "Nasty scrape. And it looks like you're getting black and blue around it. Come over here."

Ten walked over slowly and sat in front of her, placing his backpack next to the chair.

"This may sting." She poured a liquid pnto a piece of gauze she had wadded up and began cleaning his wound. She shrugged. "Not too bad. Forehead cuts always bleed a lot." She wiped over his cheekbones and around his chin while the four of them talked about the abduction.

"Do you think she let them in?" Ten wondered.

"Looks that way. Probably thought it was one of us. Easy mistake if you're not expecting anyone else."

"Not like Maria," he said. "Maybe she did know who came for her."

"Maybe," Agent Carson said.

"And I was followed," Ten said. "They must have waited outside the doctor's office while I was there. They attacked me on my way here. Again, they could have shot me but didn't."

"A warning?" one of the agents suggested.

One of the other agents, sitting behind Ten, laughed. "I don't get it; they'll kill their own men so they don't talk, but they leave us alone."

"Illegal," another agent said. "We can't trace any of the murdered ones. They don't exist. But if they kill one of us, everyone knows about it and things ramp up against them pretty damned quickly. If I were them, I'd be pretty careful too. Don't make it personal."

"The same with the girls," Ten said. "But they must get them here somehow. All these people must fly in under false pretenses." He jumped up and snapped his fingers. "Livestock crates." He pointed to the last man the nurse had been with. "Call Jacob. Check on zoo animals entering the country or… holy shit."

"What is it? What's so urgent?"

"Check trucking firms, airlines, anything delivered to or from the Exotic Animal Clinic or Dr. Afshan Shirazi. I'll bet that's where deliveries are made."

When the nurse finished, Ten rushed to his own room, rummaged through his drawers, and found an extra magazine for his gun. He went back into the living room and stuffed the third magazine into his backpack. He made sure his Glock and the other two magazines were inside. He should be prepared. All three of the agents stood around him watching as he checked things out. Agent Carson stepped closer and asked, "Where do you think you're going?"

"Nowhere yet. But as soon as we have information, I'm joining in on the takedown."

"We were told to stay here with you. To keep you here, actually."

"I don't work for you," Ten said, tightening his lips and pushing his face toward Carson. "And to make things even more interesting for you guys, that's my friend out there. I'm not sitting here and leaving her to get hurt if Jacob's big plan doesn't work. At the moment, I don't know why I ever came back here."

"Jacob knows what she means to you. He's beating himself up about letting her infiltrate this—" Abruptly, the man stopped talking.

Ten's eyes widened. "You bastards."

The agent reached for Ten, who blocked his action with his arm automatically, as though it was a punch and not a gesture of friendship. The man backstepped. "What the hell?"

One of the other agents said, "You didn't know about him?"

"Know what?" Ten questioned, even though they were talking about him.

"You're a black belt," Agent Carson said.

Ten looked at the agent who had reached toward him. He hadn't thought about what he'd done, but it was true; his training set in quickly and that's why he blocked the man who reached for him. Ten realized, maybe for the first time, that not everyone there knew who he really was or what had happened before. And he also didn't like the thought that Maria was already in on the deal and had never told him. That bit of information crashed through his skull leaving a wake. It was more important than the ignorance of these few agents. He knew, but he had to ask. "She's in on this?" And his second question, "Has she trained for it?"

"Don't get upset," one of the other agents said, as though he were in charge.

"Everyone's been lying to me," Ten said. "So why wouldn't I get upset?"

"Jacob wanted you involved. He didn't know how else to pull you in."

"Why? There's no technology going on here. No technological threat. That's my specialty, if I even have one. But that's not the issue here. The issue is that everybody has been lying to me—from start to finish. How the hell would *you* react?"

"What they're doing is a technological threat, just not the kind you're used to. Without the technology and the understanding and ability Dr. Clarkson has, this can't be done. These Humanzees wouldn't even exist."

"You all know." Ten felt sideswiped. His mind fogged over for a few seconds as the information flooded into him and then settled.

Agent Carson stepped closer to Ten and put his arm on Ten's shoulder. This time Ten didn't slap it away or block it. He waited. Carson said, "Maria was placed at MCL on purpose. She's been working the case for months. She and Jacob wanted you involved."

"And I let this happen." Ten turned away, letting Agent Carson's hand slip from his shoulder.

Two agents rushed around him to block the doorway. "The situation has changed now. We've been told not to let you go. Not yet."

Ten fumed inside, but turned around as though he were calm even under the stress of what he'd found out. He then took a breath, narrowed his eyes, and pointed toward Agent Carson. Ten laughed under his breath, lowered his arm, and headed back to his room. "I've got to think about this."

Someone closed the door to the apartment, and he heard the lock latch. The other men scuttled about behind him. He closed his bedroom door. Pissed that Maria had lied to him, that Jacob had lied to him, that everyone appeared to know what was going on but him, Ten dropped his backpack on the bed, then flopped down on it, staring at the flecked white ceiling, wondering why they'd deceived him.

CHAPTER 27

Loyalty can occur anytime during a person's life, and the loyalty Mon had for Abdi was deep, running back to childhood and, as Mon liked to believe, before childhood. With Abdi safely in a different location, Mon handled the men with greater compassion and a softer hand. He didn't want people killed; he only wanted the business to thrive. After all, he was more of a business man than a fighter of any kind. Abdi had grown up in a military family and built his business from fear and intimidation. When Mon came into the business, it was about to fail. Mon had grown up poor and no one would give him a job except Abdi. He owed the man a lot. But lately, Abdi's greed had taken over. His own fears burst through him like evil and he killed others to save himself.

Abdi had increased production, been too blatant with his actions. They were found out, somehow, and now it could be over if Mon couldn't pull things back into place quickly enough. Soon, the deliveries to America would be complete. In Iran, danger would lurk everywhere—rebellions, factions from one side or another, even retaliation from the Iranian government was a possibility.

With a heavy heart and a thrashing mind, Mon sat across from his niece, Donya, explaining they'd have to pack up the Humanzees for shipment and make the delivery early. "Then it will be their problem and not ours. But also," he added, "twenty girls."

"We're sending them back too?"

He smiled at her naiveté. "After insemination, my dear. They would be worthless to us otherwise." He lowered his chin and eyes. "Which happens tonight. I haven't decided how we will handle all this once we get home, but I will figure something out."

"Tonight? Where? We haven't prepared for any of this. How can we complete the inseminations while also preparing the Humanzees? How will Dr. Shirazi get all this done?"

"Everything will happen here, at the farm. No one will go to the clinic except to crate up the last of the young Humanzees that are there. This is our best chance of not getting caught. You will help Dr. Shirazi."

"It's still a lot of work for one night." She angled herself in her seat as though wishing to get up. "There are so few of us."

He raised his eyebrows. "There is a special treat for you."

Now she squirmed with excitement. "Really?"

"You will get to meet the great Dr. Clarkson."

She threw her hands to her chest in delight. "Finally. I thought he didn't get involved with the girls? Why is he coming this time?"

"Oh, we are requesting it. There is too much at stake and everyone has to be involved. Everyone. And he is obliging."

Her eyes narrowed and her hands dropped from her chest to her lap. Her face turned stern. "That's not like him. Not what you told me about him. You're taking him against his will."

"His wife is with child, just as he wished. He will have his son back. That was our promise to him." He looked away from his niece for a moment to shy from her disappointment. "We owe him nothing more."

"You're using her to make him train our doctors. Not her, but their son. Their unborn son."

Mon couldn't help but smile again, even though he knew his niece was unhappy with his decision. This would be a lesson to her, perhaps, that sometimes there are things of greater importance than one man's choice. "Sometimes you have to do what you must. His wife can come with him. We'll make the offer."

"Will that work? Won't everyone be in worse danger if we are found out?"

"We have to do something. We promised more than what we're delivering." Mon scratched his chin. The room closed in on him even though he glanced out the window into the bright sunlight.

"He doesn't know yet, does he?" Donya asked.

"He has told us who is following him, who has asked questions. He would not be safe if left in America. We're offering him a safe home in exchange for his knowledge."

She shook her head violently. "He's no safer here and neither are we. You'll deliver the Humanzees and the girls, which is what you get paid for." She narrowed her eyes at him again. "You will have to have another plan." It was not a question but a fact they both knew. "And there's also the truth that we couldn't use Dr. Clarkson if we left him here. He could be bought by another government, maybe his own. That's why you're kidnapping him."

"I wouldn't call it kidnapping."

"Coercing."

Mon leaned forward. "I thought you would be happy."

She tightened her lips for a moment. "I am. It will be a pleasure to meet him." Her hands fidgeted, and she adjusted her weight while sitting and the chair squeaked. "Maybe I'll get to work with him wherever we are going. I hope so. He is still a brilliant man."

Mon sat back in his chair, satisfied with how well Donya was taking the news. "I may be able to arrange that."

"Will they come after him? These Americans?" She became serene again.

Mon shook his head for his niece's sake, but he didn't know the answer to her question. It didn't matter. Once their doctors were trained, there would be no need for Dr. Clarkson, but that decision could wait.

"And Dr. Shirazi? Is he going?"

"He has been unhappy since the beginning. I'm afraid he won't go. We don't need him, after all. They are friends, but Clarkson's bargaining chips have been used up. He can't help Dr. Shirazi." He turned away again.

"You're going to kill him?"

"You know I don't like eliminating people, but he knows so much about our operation. Probably more than I can imagine. And he knows you and the others. I wouldn't put you in danger. If he should talk…"

Donya's breaths appeared to be more shallow, her shoulders slumped, and her voice lowered. "He is a nice man. I know he has been nervous about our presence. Isn't there another way?" She did not wait for an answer before she changed the subject. "So the girls will be leaving quickly, what about the youngest Humanzees? The ones here at the farm where the girls are coming tonight? And the ones I've been working with at the clinic you said would be prepared for travel. I'll get to work with them wherever we're going? Back home, I presume, for now?" He lowered his eyes for a moment. "No. You can't take them from me. Not again. Not the three that are left. Please. The research."

"We may be able to keep them for you. I am not sure yet. The ones here are young still. They are easy to transport after we crate them up. It will not be easy and will not be pretty. Some may die on the trip. It all depends on how close our adversaries come to us. We may have to destroy some of them ourselves. We can't leave them. We will deliver as many as we can. This is why we must continue. Why we must work fast."

"I couldn't destroy them. You can't ask me to do that."

"You don't have to. We have Dr. Shirazi for that. It's humane. A shot." He looked directly at her and let his hand grasp the arm of the couch. "Trust me, there is a lot of wealth at this farm. We will move as many as we can right away. If we are left alone, we may have the choice of moving some of them out over the next month or two. After the girls are gone. We'll see."

Donya stood to leave but leaned over to hug her uncle first. He patted her back and then saw her out so she could prepare for the evening. He had not told her the whole truth because he didn't know it himself. He did know they had little time to complete all their tasks. They would have to move fast.

He called one of the guards outside the door to come inside. "I am concerned over the fact that we have this Maria woman. What are we supposed to do with her? Her friends will surely come to save her. It was stupid."

The guard looked confused for a moment, then answered. "We could put her with the other girls."

Mon laughed briefly. "She is too old. We need them young. Healthy. Why Abdi allowed this to happen, I do not know." He raised a finger. "For now, we must drug her like the girls after they arrive. Keep her in a room alone. We may need a hostage. That's where she'll come in handy. Yes. This just might work in our favor. We'll take delivery this evening, do the inseminations, and have the girls in several vans to the different airstrips as usual—all before morning. I want you to oversee their travel. Keep them safe. And begin to crate the young Humanzees for shipment. The ones we can't ship we hold for a short while." He put a hand on the man's shoulder and felt the guard shake momentarily, still fearful of retribution. Another consequence of Abdi's style of control. "Now, go, spread my orders as though they are Abdi's orders, then post additional guards. We must be prepared."

"Yes, sir," the guard replied before leaving.

Mon wrung his hands together as he made his way back to his seat. Abdi had placed them under grave danger with his methods and his sloppiness, but Mon could repair the situation. That had always been his job, to think things through, and protect their assets in the end. It had happened more than once with Abdi's medical laboratories in Iran, and it would happen here as well. He loved a challenge. He was only sorry that this would be the last shipment of girls. He enjoyed his life in the States. Back in Iran, they could continue running the business, but under much greater danger. He knew Abdi would want to continue, though, as he did. Since they'd have Clarkson, production could be maintained.

Chapter 28

Of course, Ten didn't plan to stay in his apartment that evening. Since he knew the location of the farm, he pulled his backpack, all his extra magazines, and his gun together to go there and save the girls. He'd at least save the girls. If Maria were there as well, which was the most logical, then he'd save her too. But he couldn't know for sure where she was. After preparing, he walked into the kitchen and threw a few power bars and a pear into his backpack to eat on his way. He then looked in her bedroom, as though she may still be there or had been placed back there by the men who took her. Crazy.

On his return to his own room, he looked down the hall into the bathroom. A fleeting thought crossed his mind. Razor blades? He could almost smell his own blood. His preoccupation with saving Maria and the girls kept him from cutting himself. Even as the act crossed his mind, it had less weight to it. That's all he could call it. Weight. A burden. He turned away to follow his original plan. He threw his backpack over his shoulder, partially unzipped to make it easy to get to his pistol, which he'd carry with him once he arrived near the farm. As he left his bedroom, someone knocked at the door, and announced his name. Agent Connor.

Ten opened the door and Agent Connor stood outside slightly behind Dr. Shirazi. "What's he doing here?" Ten asked.

"He wants protection, but also wanted to see you," Agent Connor said. Then he pointed toward Ten's backpack. "I thought you were staying in while we took care of this?"

"I can't stay cooped up. Just going to take a drive."

"Oh. Well, now you have company. Should I stay?"

Ten cocked his head toward Dr. Shirazi. "I'm sure it's a friendly visit. And you'll be around if I need you."

"I'm available. There are five of us now. We'll watch the building."

Somehow, Ten wasn't so sure five would be any more effective than the three who guarded the building before. If the amateur kidnappers could get past three of them, then why would five be any different? The whole thing, both sides, reeked of talentless employees, a comedy. "Was he trailed?" Ten asked Agent Connor.

Connor shook his head no.

"I can't stay long," Shirazi said. "I have to be somewhere."

Connor shoved him inside. "We know where you have to be."

Dr. Shirazi tripped into the apartment as Ten stepped aside. "The farm outside of town," Ten said.

"How do you know?"

Ten led Shirazi into the kitchen area and pointed to one of the stools near the counter. Shirazi pitched himself atop the stool, a quizzical look on his face.

Ten glanced at Connor. "You decided to stay?"

"For now. I changed my mind." He shrugged. "Call it curiosity."

Ten turned back to Shirazi. "We know a lot more about this case than you might think. For example, Clarkson can't be trusted. The girls will be delivered for insemination tonight. We know what you're going to do afterward..."

"I don't even know that."

"We do," Ten lied. "So why don't you tell us why you're here?"

Shirazi looked nervous and scared. "I shouldn't have come here. If they knew…"

"We'll protect you the best we can," Ten assured him.

He glanced around the room like a frightened animal looking for the quickest way out. "Clarkson is my friend, *was* my friend, but he can't be trusted any longer. After the death—"

"His son," Ten said impatiently.

"Yes. And now with Karla pregnant—"

"He thinks he's finished with them. But they're not finished with him," Ten said. "Doesn't he realize that?"

"His abilities are very specific. Only he knows…"

"Then they have no recourse. If they are going to continue on…"

"I heard that they are taking the Humanzees from the clinic. They're leaving." Fear showed in Shirazi's eyes. "That means they're taking the ones from the farm too."

"From the farm?" Ten couldn't hold back his surprise. "I hadn't thought of that."

"They only keep them for a few years, then ship them out. The ones at the clinic are experiments in cognitive understanding, psychological studies, that sort of thing. At the farm, they have infants to about two years old. But that's not why I'm here. It's after tonight…"

"They won't need you anymore. They only need him, Dr. Clarkson," Ten said.

"We were good, good friends, but he can't protect me if they take him. They've killed," Shirazi said. "I've heard how ruthless they are."

"They even killed one of your Humanzees the other night."

"You know that?" Shirazi appeared surprised and so did Agent Connor.

"You keep saying they," Connor broke in.

"I've never met who is in charge. Only their researchers."

"Researchers? The ones who study the Humanzees at the clinic?" Ten asked.

"When this first started, the Humanzees didn't live very long. Carl still didn't have everything down, all the right techniques, the right technologies. He passed his work through MCL so he could control what came to me. Karla would keep certain evidence, certain samples. She'd do tests and then pass the rest on. Eventually, she held back one of the inseminations. Hers. The Humanzees inseminations would most often take place at the clinic, then be transferred to the farm. Carl would not touch the chimpanzees and brought me into this. He didn't want to be a part of this, except that he needed the time and money for the research he needed for his own purposes."

"And now you want out," Ten said.

"You said it. They don't need me. When it's over…"

"You're over," Connor said out loud.

"You going to do this last job for them?" Ten asked.

"I must."

"What do you want from us?"

"Protection. Tell your men I'm not one of them. Don't kill me and don't let them kill me. That's all I ask." He looked from one to the other of them. "I'll testify."

Agent Connor rested his hands on his hips as he spoke. "You thought you were bringing information and could hold out if we didn't say yes to your request, but we know what's going on and plan to stop this before the inseminations even begin. We know more than you."

Shirazi stared at Ten, who turned around to talk with Agent Connor. "All five of you need to watch him while I'm gone. He's going nowhere." He held his hand toward Shirazi and wiggled his fingers. "Car keys."

Shirazi reluctantly handed him his keys. "The dark green 4Runner. If I don't show up tonight, they'll know something's wrong."

"We'll get to them before that." Under the present circumstances, Ten figured Maria would be at the farm. Where else could they take her at this point?

"I can't let you leave," Agent Connor said. "My orders—"

"Have been changed. You can contact Jacob and he'll tell you that I don't work for you. You can't order me around and you can't hold me without due cause." Ten slipped the backpack from his shoulder, reached inside, and pulled out his Glock, sliding the safety off as he did so. He pointed the gun at Connor. "And… I have a gun." He raised his eyebrows.

"You won't shoot me."

Ten shrugged and swung the gun toward Shirazi, who jumped from his seat, raised his hands into the air, and stood perfectly still. "He's a criminal. I can shoot him," Ten said.

"I'll call Jacob, but I don't like this and neither will he." Then he added, "You're crazy as shit sometimes."

"Glad you noticed." Ten waited for the agent to make the call, talk with Jacob, and contact the other agents watching the building.

"He said to stay low," Agent Connor said. "They expect to retrieve the girls before they reach the farm."

"That's the plan. But what about Maria?"

"He didn't mention her."

Ten replaced his gun into the backpack and walked out. He passed the other agents in the hallway as he left. None of them said a word. One nodded in acknowledgement. Ten nodded back.

Outside, he punched the button on the 4Runner's key fob. Lights flashed and a horn blew nearby. He walked over to the SUV and climbed inside. The inside of the vehicle smelled of wet dog mixed with bird, cat, and he couldn't tell what else. Yeah, it was an exotic animal clinic, but the smells were pretty much like all animals. He started the car. Time for a little drive.

Chapter 29

Maria wiggled to get free as the men pulled the hood from her head and shoved her into an empty room. Even walking to the room, Maria could smell the house. The odors were old and the building felt heavy, strong; a big house with many rooms. Judging by the thick baseboards and wallpapered walls, her assessment seemed confirmed. An old four-poster bed sat near one wall, a single window had been boarded up, and a lone lamp sat on a bedside table. The rest of the room was empty, the walls bare. The bed had been freshly made. She paced the room for a few minutes and stood near the boarded-up window when the door latch clicked. The sound caused her to shiver. What would they want with her now? She held her ground near the boarded-up window and heard the lock click a second time. The door opened. Dr. Clarkson looked around it, walked into the room, and closed the door behind him, leaning against it as though holding others back from entering.

"You going to let me out of here?" Maria asked.

He gave her a little grin. "Not quite, my dear."

"Then what do you want?"

"Who do you work for?"

"Excuse me?"

"You were placed at MCL to spy on my wife, to find out what she was up to. So who do you work for?" He tapped on the door behind him and she heard it latch from the outside. He walked farther into the room. "They have ways to find this out. I thought I'd offer an easier chance for you to come clean. I don't have to be so kind as to ask, and since you were spying on my wife, maybe I shouldn't." His voice changed with his last statement.

That was the Dr. Clarkson she knew from meeting him at the Exotic Animal Clinic. That was the rude, uncaring sound she knew was his true self. "I'm sure they could torture me, but why would they? It's no secret to them, probably. Do you really think we haven't been watching you for a long time? This whole operation is carried on by a bunch of buffoons. You might be brilliant"—she gave him that—"but they aren't."

"You're lying," he said.

Maria cocked her head. "Really? How long have I been working at MCL?" When he didn't answer right away, she said, "Ask Karla." Then she narrowed her eyes and said, "They'll be coming for me."

"Stop stalling. No one is coming for you. Not yet. And when they do, we're ready. Especially that partner of yours. We'll kill him first."

"You bought into all this?" She didn't wait for an answer; instead, she pursed her lips. "You couldn't hurt Ten any more than he hurts himself." She squinted in Clarkson's direction and walked closer to him. "When someone doesn't care if he lives or dies, he is much more dangerous."

Dr. Clarkson blinked. "I'll ask one more time."

"You want to know who's behind this?" He didn't respond. His arrogance could be seen in his face. Maria knew it would make no difference, so she told him. It wasn't a secret. "The International Security for Technological Innovations."

"Never heard of it."

She shrugged. "They've heard of you. And that's all that matters."

"What do they want with us? To shut us down? My research has created a new race." He leaned toward her, his chin thrust out, "I should get a Nobel Prize. This has never been done before." He banged his fist against his chest. "I did it! No one else!" His voice softened. "Why do they always wish to shut down the scientist making the most progress?"

"Through foreign money," she said.

"Because the American government wouldn't support the research!"

She was a scientist too, and understood—to the heart— exactly what he was saying. "But the girls you're trafficking. You can't ruin their lives for this."

"Ruin!" He spun around and paced along the wall, never looking at her. "Those girls would be killed if not for us. These rebels murder young girls so they can't produce more enemies. We're saving them. We're introducing them to a life they could never have."

"It's wrong," she said. "Against their will."

"Then we should let them die? Is that how you would have it?"

His words confused her for a moment. Was he right? No, she couldn't let him into her head. "You kidnap them. You take them from their families."

"And we save their lives. They produce one offspring for us. That's all we ask." He shrugged. "Maybe more."

"Then you send them back," she affirmed. "And then they are killed, captured, tortured, sold."

His back was to her. "That is not my concern."

Back to square one. "Well, it is mine. It is ours," she said, trying to include ISTI, make her objection more important. "Save them if you want, but don't save them just so you can use them your own way. And then return them to a worse fate."

"Your government doesn't care about the girls, only about the technology, the science behind what I'm doing. They wish to make their own monsters."

"They are not monsters," she said.

He smiled. "You've seen them, then. I was told someone had broken into the clinic. Now we know who it was. I suppose your friend was there as well." He shook his head as though it was too bad.

"They're children. Aren't you afraid your own son…" She stopped talking as soon as he turned to face her, his eyes blaring with fire.

"You don't get to mention my son. With the right machinery and enough money…" He didn't have to finish his sentence.

"I'm sorry," she said, trying to calm the situation.

"You'll be escorted to where we take the girls. Shirazi will deal with you tonight."

Maria knew what he meant by that, that she was going to become one of them, but she was too old for that. They needed young girls, strong girls. "You can't," she said.

"It has nothing to do with you. We can do whatever we like. All we have to do is avoid your little security group for another day or two. They couldn't possibly stop every one of our shipments."

"Why are you so involved in this? What happened? You have what you wanted."

"Yes, I have—*we* have—our son back. Soon enough. But my research, it has taken on its own need. I want to see it through. The Humanzees in the clinic, from what I'm told, are doing extremely well. Proof that the ones here will live longer and be teachable. I have some final adjustments I wish to make. You have no idea what I can do with the right equipment, the right tools. This could open, beyond belief, the whole study of DNA, how to manipulate it, use it to create…" He shook his head at her as though he were wasting his time. "And I did it." he said with a smirk.

"You've become attached more to your work than your family."

"There is more to do."

"And Karla? Your son?"

"They will be with me as I discover how to create life, new life, original life. There is so much to do, so much to learn."

The more he talked, the more his eyes appeared crazed to her. Maria didn't know how to respond. He had checked out. He lived in his own world. When that may have happened, when his brain clicked over, who could tell? She'd heard of scientists getting so involved in their work that they'd rather die than stop. And here it was, before her very eyes, a madman, a genius. What could he do? She couldn't believe that the men he relied on would let him continue his research without it being profitable, and she knew the US government probably wouldn't fund his research unless it became top secret and overly controlled. She couldn't see Clarkson allowing that. Her mind rolled around the possibilities. And maybe that was it; her way in. She strolled closer to him, held out her hands. "You have no idea, do you?"

His face became alert, as did his body. He stepped closer but didn't reach out. "How do you mean that?"

"You know about Area 51, don't you? That's where important research is being done every day. Your kind of research. Plus, I can't say this for sure, but if they do have aliens…"

He shook his head as though he had cobwebs inside. "I can't believe that. Why haven't they contacted me?"

"Because we needed to stop this operation first? If these people found out…"

He lowered his head and paced in thought. She had him. It was a long shot, but maybe he'd create his own assumptions using her lead in. "You don't need them any longer," she said quietly. "We've spent all this time following you. To see what you're doing. Its importance. Well, now you have us."

Chapter 30

The evening would come on slower than Ten would like, and he knew it, so he took his time, pulled off the highway, and stopped for a late dinner at a truck stop. The greasy food went down smoothly—meatloaf, potatoes, and green beans—but didn't settle well once it got there. Maybe he should have eaten a power bar instead. He had been eating a lot more than usual. Stress, perhaps. He had a few cups of coffee during his meal, thought about how bizarrely his life had played out, and how many people had died over the past year or so, and finally ordered dessert after the waitress asked him if he needed anything else for the third time. Eventually, he paid the bill, left a hefty tip, and wandered out to the 4Runner feeling full.

Night settled in easily as he drove through the country. Somehow the air, the wind coming through the window, the silence, helped him to forget, for a short time, what he had gone through and where he was now. How many people had he killed? How many had been killed around him?

As he got closer to the farm where the girls would be delivered, he slowed and drove past the huge, mansion-like farmhouse. A multigenerational home, as each generation had attached another section to the original farmhouse. Layer by layer, it grew to what it now was, a mansion with edges belying how it arrived in that state.

The windows open, Shirazi's car was finally starting to smell better. Field grass rose along the road, trees grew in groves between houses. A mile down the road, Ten pulled the 4Runner onto a dirt road and then immediately off-road into a small opening between two trees. He got out, dragging his backpack behind him. He locked the car with another beep and clunk after punching the key fob. He wondered how anyone could be sneaky anymore with all the noises the new cars made. He walked toward the main road, but cut off before reaching it. He stayed just inside the woods and arrived at the farmhouse in about a half hour. Darkness obscured his whereabouts even though the farmhouse remained in dim light. A lot of lights were on inside as well. Some windows were boarded up, while others weren't. A long, low barn, like a pig barn, sat a thousand feet from the main house. There were lights on in the barn too.

As much as he had planned to sit and observe for a while, Ten couldn't sit still and walked around the property the best he could. At one point, he left the woods and ran along a small creek, bent over as close to the ground as he could, and ducked behind one of several outbuildings also occupying the property. From there he snuck up on the pig barn, which had a row of windows along its longest side. It was closed up pretty tightly on the end he could see and looked as though it had been recently refurbished.

He saw only one guard walking around the back of the building and waited for him to disappear around the corner. He waited another ten minutes and the same man came back around, walked the length of one side, then disappeared again.

Ten had at least eight minutes, so he ran to the barn and looked into the window along one side. The place was laid out like a hospital, with equipment sitting on traveling racks, and shelves lined with medicine. Some counters were littered with test tubes and chemicals. A long row of beds ran down the middle of the space, with equipment racks with plastic tubes sitting next to them like you'd find in a hospital ward in a war zone. Along one side, there appeared to be separate rooms with doors, like exam rooms. This was the place. He straightened and strained to count the beds when he saw someone inside looking at him. Before he knew it, the man pulled a walkie talkie to his lips. Ten spun around to run but the other guard stood near the other end of the building with a pistol aimed at him.

"I wouldn't," the man said in a heavy accent.

Ten kept his backpack on his shoulder but raised his hands into the air. "I was just hiking and—"

"Shut up. Nobody hikes here in the dark. Now, slide the backpack to the ground and put your hands back into the air."

Ten used his left hand to slide his backpack over his right shoulder. While doing so, he noticed the other guard, who was inside the barn a moment ago, walking up behind him. "Easy," Ten said. "I'm just a hiker."

"Move away," the guard with the gun said, still walking toward Ten.

Ten took two steps to the side to give them room to get close to the backpack. Not something he looked forward to.

"Farther," the man said, waving his gun.

Ten responded as asked. The other guard picked up the backpack and removed Ten's Glock. There was a magazine in the pistol. "Not just a hiker."

The guard from inside used his walkie talkie to call someone else. Ten listened as the person who answered told the men, "This man is dangerous, we'll send help." He liked the sound of that. He *was* dangerous, and all one of these men had to do was get close enough and he'd prove it.

One guard stood in front of him and one to the side, both with pistols pointed at him.

"I'm really not that dangerous," Ten said.

"Shut up," the guard in front of him said.

After only a few minutes, two other men showed up, each with a pistol of his own. One carried a black hood, which he placed over Ten's head, probably to distract him.

Then his hands were tied with thick wire ties. He heard them being zipped into place, could feel the plastic against his skin. He could get out of those, but it would take some stretching, and it would hurt. Then one of the men shoved him in the direction of the farmhouse. He had no idea how many of the guards followed him to the house, but he suspected only the two who had come to the rescue. The other two probably went back to their duties guarding the pig barn, waiting for the arrival of the girls.

While being shoved every few minutes toward the house, he realized that his interest in the pig barn was probably a warning to those in charge that people were onto them. He worried that they might postpone the delivery. He couldn't be sure, of course. They were probably running scared about now anyway. The truth was, at the moment, it didn't matter what he thought or what they did. He had to pay attention to where they were taking him. He had to listen for Maria.

Someone opened the farmhouse door and shoved Ten inside. With every shove, Ten tripped, then regained his equilibrium. He was forced up some stairs and eventually shoved into a room. He heard a gasp the moment he entered.

Maria.

CHAPTER 31

Mon paced in the living room while Dr. Clarkson sat comfortably in an overstuffed chair. On one of his rounds behind the sofa, Mon glared at Clarkson, "You're not worried?"

Clarkson turned his head toward Mon. "You had me scared at the beginning, you and Abdi with all your threats, but you need me more than I need you. It took a while for me to realize that, but it's true. Now, with this tech security group on your ass, you're the ones running scared. And honestly, that's not my problem."

"You're in on this, aren't you? You must be."

"Not at all."

"Then you must know that they'll arrest you too. You're not safe with them either," Mon said.

"I was coerced into this. My life and my family were at stake. They won't blame me." He turned his head away slowly. "I'm a medical genius. I see that now. The medical community won't let the American government put me away."

"They won't finance your research either," Mon said, hoping to set Clarkson straight.

"I didn't think about it before, but you're wrong. The US has many secret areas where they study sciences the public is not ready to hear about. I'm starting to believe my research won't stop, no matter who pays for it." He laughed. "I'm over the hump, you might say. What I've learned, what

I know, can change how we populate the universe, not just Earth."

Mon walked into Clarkson's view. The man had gotten too full of himself. "You find this amusing?"

Clarkson didn't show signs of agreement or disagreement. "I'm just saying that I don't have to be worried. That it's your worry, not mine. Besides, you need me to be calm in case Shirazi doesn't show up."

"He'll show up."

"He's late. He's never late. Either they have him or he's trying to escape. Who can blame him?"

Mon hadn't thought that Shirazi would try to escape. He was a countryman. What about loyalty to the cause, the country? And in a moment, Mon knew the answer to his question. Abdi. The man had scared everyone with his control tactics and now look at the situation they were in. He spun around and addressed a guard standing near the doorway. "Bring Abdi here. Tell him it's safe."

Now Clarkson sat up, more alert.

Mon pointed a finger at him. "You didn't expect me to do that, did you?"

"What's going on?"

"I love my friend, but he got us into this. And perhaps only he can get us out of it. Even you respond to him and he isn't here yet." Mon surprised himself with his change of heart, but he thought now of his family, of the greater plan, the money involved, the eventual freedom it would buy—but only if everything went as planned. The program had to be finished. Abdi had control, and Mon had plans. He knew things were getting out of hand. As much as he felt like he could get them out of their predicament, things were changing too quickly. Abdi would instill military tactics, harsh, but the work would get done. If one man from the American's security group knew where they were, then all of them did.

"Abdi will kill everyone, including you," Clarkson said. Mon shook his head. "He's dangerous if pushed. He'd let every one of us get killed to save his own ass." Mon saw Clarkson's hands shaking. His knees seemed weak as he stood up.

"I have your attention now, do I?" Mon said. "So, you thought you could fool me into thinking you didn't care, that you weren't afraid."

"I just want to continue with my research, protect my family. I want things to be back to normal."

"Ah, your tune has changed so quickly. Well, that will never happen." He glanced at his watch. "Shirazi isn't coming. You're going to do the inseminations. You're going to need an assistant. My niece, Donya, will help you."

"She's a vet assistant, not a—"

"That's who you'll be working with! She has assisted Dr. Shirazi on numerous occasions. She has always wanted to work with you." He lowered his chin and raised his eyes. "And if you are rude to her, I will kill you myself." Before Clarkson could respond, Mon took the few steps toward him and shoved him in the chest, forcing him back into his chair.

Clarkson didn't look very happy and that's exactly what Mon wanted. Standing at the window, Mon felt overjoyed to see a van pulling down the driveway toward the house. He rushed out of the living room to greet them at the front door. Three men followed him. Mon jogged from the porch to the drive, greeted the driver, and asked about trouble.

"Nothing for us, but one of the other vans was abducted, maybe five girls, the smaller van."

"They know where we are," Mon said. He turned to one of the men who had followed him outside. "I want more guards at the end of the drive, walking the periphery near the woods, protecting the insemination building. The other vans are to go directly to the lab. I want everyone to have machine guns and pistols. If anything looks wrong, shoot on sight."

"We don't have enough machine guns to go around."

Mon felt the pushback from the guard. He wanted to be left in charge, but only Abdi had their respect. Perhaps that was the only way. He screamed at the man. "You are in charge of stopping them. You decide how this goes now. Either kill them or capture them, but we must finish this job and get out fast."

The driver got back into the vehicle and drove over to the insemination building to unload as the guard quickly shuffled off toward the house.

Mon stood alone outside, the other men gone to take care of their duties. Before going back inside, a black Lincoln came down the drive toward him. Abdi. It stopped and the big man got out of the car, a pistol in his hand, pointing at Mon. "I heard what's happening. Why did you call for me? I thought you had this big plan."

"Protection," Mon said without thinking. He didn't like the gun pointing in his direction. It had never bothered him before, but today… "They appear to know what we're doing. You know we captured the man who worked with Maria?"

"I heard." He lowered the pistol.

"If they know where we are, they may have known where you were, and you weren't protected there. Not like here." He opened his arms wide. "We have full firepower here."

"These idiots." Abdi pushed past Mon and Mon felt a sudden sense of uselessness. "I have this under control!" he yelled after his boss.

"No, you don't. You've let things slip. Where's Shirazi?"

"Late."

Abdi swung around and pointed the gun at Mon for the second time. "He's not coming," Abdi said with anger in his voice. He nodded. "You are too soft. Where are the girl and the man?"

"Upstairs." Mon rushed after Abdi, who headed straight for the stairs. "If you kill them, we have no bargaining…"

Abdi didn't even turn.

Mon followed behind him, protesting, but getting no response.

Down the hall, two guards stood in front of the door where Ten and Maria were located. Abdi waved them aside, walked inside—Mon on his heels—and shot Maria the moment he entered the room fully.

Chapter 32

Ten rushed toward Maria and caught her before she crumpled to the ground. Blood spread on her blouse along her side where a hole had torn through. He had no idea what the bullet may have ripped apart inside her. He scooped her body loosely into his arms and laid her on the bed. She moaned and opened her mouth to speak, "The girls," she said.

Ten placed a finger over his lips to quiet her. "I know." Even after being shot, she thought of others. Ten felt a wrench of guilt in his stomach, but for only a second before he addressed the large, dark man who'd shot as he rushed into the room with a gun in his fat grip. Ten would have jumped him if he weren't on the wrong side of the bed.

The man seemed unaffected by Maria's condition. Pointing the gun at Ten, he said, "You! How much do you know?" A second man came in behind the first and stood near the doorway as though he were frightened to enter completely. The shadow of one guard, also holding a gun, stood in the hallway.

Three of them, as far as Ten could tell. A second shot rang out and chips flew from the wall behind him.

"How much?" the man yelled again.

Ten raged inside while remaining calm on the outside. A familiar feeling. Fearless rage. He recognized it, even though he didn't know where it came from. He walked toward the bottom of the bed while he talked. "It's hard to know how much I know when I don't know how much there is in total."

"Stop where you are." Another bullet split more sheetrock from the wall near him.

Ten raised his hands, but kept walking, now past the bottom of the bed, toward the man holding the gun. "I don't talk until someone helps her."

"I don't need you," the big man said.

Just then, the man who'd followed him into the room said, "We need a hostage. If she dies…"

Ten turned his gaze toward the other man. "If she dies, you're both dead."

The big man laughed as though Ten had made a joke. Out of what Ten could only imagine was cocky confidence, the man glanced over at his associate with a smirk still on his face.

And that's when Ten leaped at the pistol. Not to grab it, but to slam the back of the man's hand with his knuckles, knowing that the trigger would be pulled while doing so. There was no telling where that bullet would go, but Ten knew the slight kick would help to loosen the man's grip and, most likely, the gun would fall to the floor. Ten had no doubt he was faster than the man he attacked. The only question was, how fast was the guard?

As planned, an instant later, the big man's gun fired and Ten felt something rip through the skin of his hip. But the gun was down. Ten landed flat near the big man's foot, reached for the pistol with one hand, and slammed the man in the groin with the closed fist of his other hand. While the man toppled, Ten rolled away, raised the pistol between the man's legs, and shot the guard, who dropped to the floor.

The man who followed the big man into the room didn't appear to be armed. But a second guard Ten had not seen stepped into the room and took a blind shot. Ten was already pulling the big man in front of him and heard a grunt when the man got hit.

The second man in the room yelled, "Abdi!" and ran for the big man. Ten didn't care. He shot over the man's shoulder and hit the other guard in the neck, toppling him to the hardwood floor.

By now, a lot of noise rang out in the hallway. Ten grabbed the second man's shirt, lifted him to his feet and held the gun to his jaw. The next man into the room stopped abruptly.

"Get a doctor up here. Now," Ten ordered. The new man in the room stared for a moment at the man Ten held at gunpoint. Ten said, "I know Clarkson is in the house. I want him up here taking care of Maria. Go!"

The man Ten held a gun to nodded and the new person ran off, yelling something in another language to those in the hall, reducing the overall noises being made by a lot. "You cannot make it out alive," said the man.

Ten pressed the gun hard into the man's cheek. "I don't have to; she does."

"I can help you. We can bargain. My name is Mon. I am in charge."

Ten pulled the man closer toward the bed. "Maria!" Her eyes opened. "Stay with me. Clarkson's coming."

Clarkson walked gingerly into the room, saw Maria on the bed, and rushed toward her. Even if Ten thought he was a jerk, he suddenly acted like a doctor as he took charge and yelled for one of the guards to get his medical kit. He stood and addressed Mon. "You've made quite a mess of this, haven't you?"

Mon didn't respond.

"Is this guy really the boss here?" Ten asked.

"He's second in command, if you will," Clarkson said. "The man on the floor over there. He was in charge." He glanced into Ten's eyes for only a moment, almost as though asking a question. "I'll have to get to him in a minute."

"You knew all along," Ten said, realizing how integral Clarkson really was to the operation.

A young woman came into the room wearing a lab coat and carrying what looked like an antique medical kit. Her dark complexion matched that of the others, except for Clarkson, whose pale skin almost glowed in the room. She stared at Clarkson and Maria for a moment, then turned and addressed Mon. "Uncle?"

"Do what is necessary, Donya. I'll be alright."

"Unless she dies," Ten said. "Then no one's alright."

Donya quickly turned back to Clarkson and opened the bag. She kneeled next to it to pull out whatever Clarkson asked for.

Maria's curly hair looked damp and her face moist. She had not moved since Ten set her on the bed, but she was conscious, which was a positive sign.

Clarkson touched Donya's shoulder, "Here's your chance." He looked toward Ten one more time. "It's not good, but I'll do what I can."

"You'll stay with her and out of my way," Ten said while shoving Mon in front of him.

"I'll work on him as soon as I'm done here," Clarkson said, pointing toward Abdi again, as though letting Mon know he was still part of their team.

Ten didn't buy it, but then, he didn't have to; Mon did. He pulled the pistol from Mon's jaw, pointed it at Abdi's head, and pulled the trigger. The body jerked a few times and went still, collapsing even further onto the floor. Ten looked directly at Clarkson. "You will save her life or you'll die." Ten shoved the now trembling Mon into the hall. Several men with guns had gathered outside, one down the hall to his left and two to his right, where the stairs lay. "You won't shoot me as long as I have Mon, so you can either drop your weapons and let me pass or I'll kill each of you individually and then kill this man."

The weapons dropped.

This time when he shoved Mon into the hall, he felt his hip burn. He looked down and saw blood on his pants. He could still walk fine, but the wound was starting to hurt like hell. He turned Mon toward the stairs, then held him with the gun scrunched into the man's cheek, shoving hard against his cheekbone. "You two kick those guns over the ledge, then get down the hall to my left." He looked at the man to his left. "You can kick your gun toward me." After two guns were heard hitting the floor below and the other gun was close enough for Ten to pick up, he bent down slowly and grabbed the second gun and shoved it under his belt in the back. He never took his pistol off of Mon. "Now open one of those doors and go into the room," he told them. "Close the door and lock it. When I hear the click, I'll leave."

A moment later, the door lock clicked and Ten shoved Mon down the hallway toward the stairs. "You'd better hope your people are not stupid."

CHAPTER 33

Ten followed Mon downstairs. A guard near the doorway to the living room stepped out and Ten shot him in the chest, letting him crumple to the ground. When another man came through the front door, Ten yelled for him to halt. "Drop your gun and tell the others to do the same."

"There are no others."

"Bullshit."

"They're all at the insemination building with the girls."

"Then back away," Ten said. He glanced down to see that his phone was missing from his shirt pocket. It must have fallen out while he wrestled with the men upstairs. He wasn't sure what to do. Even with Mon as his hostage, he suspected there were too many of them at the insemination building. But he had no choice. He shoved Mon ahead of him while the other guard led the way. It suddenly felt like a long hundred yards to the pig barn.

Before they were all the way to the barn, another van drove down the driveway. Ten took a deep breath and shoved Mon faster, not knowing what to expect. It looked as though the van was headed for the house first. In his haste, Ten didn't see the three men flanking him until it was too late. One of them yelled out and shot into the air for Ten to stop moving.

Ten glanced over his shoulder and saw one of the men from the van running toward him. Instincts took over as he grabbed the second pistol from his belt, dropped to the ground, rolled, and shot two of the three guards who had flanked him. Mon rushed forward, but tripped and fell, which gave the last guard from the barn open air to fire at Ten. The bullet grazed the ground near Ten's chest. The man behind him fired as well, this time hitting him in the leg. Before either of them got off a second round, Ten shot the man behind him, rolled again, and shot toward the last guard from the barn. He missed, but the man dropped anyway.

Ten swung around. Three agents ran toward him. Jacob walked casually behind them.

"You stupid son of a bitch," Jacob said when he got close enough for Ten to hear.

The agents ran past Ten toward the pig barn. One other shot was fired, but that was all. "Maria got shot," Ten said. "She's upstairs in the house."

Jacob swung around and gave orders to call an ambulance and to check on Maria. When he turned back around to Ten, he knelt down and reached to pull Ten's pant leg up and over Ten's calf. "I think you'll make it." Then his expression changed, and he reached toward the other patch of blood coming from Ten's hip. "What the hell happened?"

"Grazed. It burns, but it's fine." He moved Jacob's hand away. "Maria…"

"Yeah, yeah, we're on it. They'll take care of her."

"Clarkson's up there."

"Good, you have a built-in doctor. Now, what about these girls?" He stood up and reached for Ten's hand. Ten shoved one pistol into his belt and let Jacob help him up. Holding to Jacob, Ten hobbled the rest of the way to the barn. When he walked inside, two agents stood around a dozen or more girls, who sat quietly on the beds. A few of the doors were open to the rooms along the side. The cries of children rang through the building as well. Some of the girls didn't look as though they had any idea what was about to happen, while others appeared drugged. He asked Jacob, "What about the other girls on their way?"

"There were three vans in all. We stopped two before they got here. All the girls, and men, are in custody. We'll take care of these girls too."

"What about the Humanzees?"

"We're working on that. It appears as though they've shipped some to Iran, ones that are older than about six months old. The mortality rate was high for a while, that's why they studied the ones in Shirazi's clinic, trying to figure out why those lived longer. You can hear there are some here too."

"How many do you think are in Iran? How many in all?"

Jacob didn't answer right away, then took a deep breath. "Nearly two hundred."

Ten shook his head. "What are you going to do next?"

"First, we stop it from continuing."

"Done," Ten said.

"Now, we try to find the thread that binds all of this together and follow that. It's not so easy. We'll need to incorporate other divisions, maybe the CIA, who knows who else."

"It's going to get dirty," Ten said.

"Yes, but it's not technical now, it's biological, so it's not our problem. Believe me, there are whole divisions involved in the trafficking operations. They were a big help on this as you can imagine."

"And these girls?"

Jacob shook his head. "Well, I hate to say it, but I promised Maria—"

"Go no further," Ten said.

"Shall we see how she's doing?" Jacob swung Ten around and helped him hobble back toward the house. Before they were halfway, an agent brought medical gear to stop the bleeding, which had slowed on its own already. Another two agents took over Jacob's role in helping Ten get the rest of the way to the house.

When he entered the upstairs room, Maria lay awake. She turned her head and smiled at Ten. Clarkson stood and stepped to the side. Maria reached out and Ten limped over to take her hand. "You saved the girls," he said.

"You did. I knew you'd be the one to do it."

"I had to, once I got started."

"I know," she said, "that's how you are." She took a deep breath and Clarkson touched Ten on the wrist. He let go of her hand.

"She'll make it," Clarkson said.

Ten nodded and told her to rest. He left the room and met Jacob in the hallway. "She's never getting involved again."

Jacob laughed. "They told me that you know she's part of the team already. Besides, you know she has her own mind."

"You don't have to keep her on."

He smiled. "Don't worry. I get the feeling she'll be working with these girls for a while. She has to recuperate. You'll have time to convince her to quit. Although, I don't think you can."

"What do you think will happen to the Humanzees?"

"I can't say yet. All different departments will get involved now. I suspect Maria will be in the thick of it for a while, since she'll be involved with the girls."

"Good," Ten said. "It'll keep her out of trouble."

"What about you?"

Ten knew what Jacob was asking, but he didn't have an answer yet.

THE END

About the Author

Terry Persun has been writing and publishing poetry, short stories, and novels since the early 1970s. He has been the recipient of many novel and poetry awards over the years, including the Star of Washington Award, a Silver IPPY for historical fiction, two Book of the Year finalist awards in the science fiction category, two finalist awards from the USA Book News International Book Awards (one in science fiction and one in historical fiction), two poetry chapbook awards, and a Jeanne Voge Poetry Award. Terry writes in a variety of genres, including science fiction, thriller, mystery, and mainstream fiction. His Doublesight novels were selected as a Kindle World for fan-fiction writers. He is a respected keynoter and speaker at libraries, writers' groups, writers' conferences, and universities across the country. Terry has an MA in creative writing from SUNY Stony Brook.